ZODIAC DRAGON BROTHERHOOD

LEGACY OF FIRE

USA TODAY BESTSELLING AUTHOR

GENEVIEVE JACK

Legacy of Fire: Zodiac Dragon Brotherhood

Copyright © Genevieve Jack 2023

Published by Carpe Luna, Ltd. Bloomington, IL 61704

Second Edition: June 2025

ISBN: 978-1-962757-09-6

eISBN: 978-1-962757-08-9

v 1.0

A legacy of war. A legacy of love. A legacy of fire.

Starting over sucks, but as a Pisces dragon shifter, I go where the Oracle tells me. Right now, the stars say Mason Forge needs to be here, slinging coffee in rural Virginia, which means my dragon energy is meant to inspire one of the human residents. Sure, I'd prefer to be a defender of my race like my father, but the Zodiac Brotherhood plays a limited role since the peace accord with the Saint's Order—the secret society that traditionally hunted my kind.

The moment I meet Reagan, I know she's the reason the stars have guided me to Thornsboro, but the specifics of her secret project are a mystery. When she finally trusts me enough to share that she's investigating the Saint's Order, I'm horrified. I've been unwittingly helping her uncover the one story that could be a critical threat to my kind. To make things right, I have to leave her. Only, my dragon has chosen Reagan as his mate, and with my inner beast calling the shots, staying away is no longer an option.

Chapter One

MASON

Trusting the universe seems like a good idea until you actually have to do it. Take my word for it. I'm no spiritual guru or anything, but as a dragon living among humans, the philosophy is personal. In theory, my kind believe there's a great, benevolent creator who sent us to Earth to help humanity reach its ultimate potential. We're here to inspire. It's said that a dragon like me was there when man lit their first fire, carved their first wheel, and flipped their first kingdom.

I guess I buy into all that. I mean, the inspiration part is verifiably true. But the motivation of the one we call the creator? That's something else entirely.

Let's just say, I'm not always confident the stars have my best interests at heart.

Especially a few months ago when our Oracle sent

me to the tiny town of Thornsboro, Virginia, to run a coffeehouse. I didn't know then how everything that would happen would change our world. I didn't know that I'd be the first to feel the shifting tides.

But I'm getting ahead of myself.

My transition to Thornsboro hadn't gone smoothly. I'd spent the early days evicting a family of raccoons from the air ducts of my new cafe and had moved on to scrubbing three generations of filth from the counter seating. The place was a mess. If a health inspector had ever visited the previous owner, there certainly weren't any signs of those visits. Based on the state of the kitchen alone, it's a miracle he died of a heart attack and not typhoid or food poisoning.

The place had some regulars, but none of them were scientists on the verge of major breakthroughs, or humanitarians in need of financing to save a community. This town was more about rocking chairs, family farms, and remote work. Nothing wrong with that. Just not the place you usually find a dragon.

"She doesn't make mistakes," my uncle Connor said into my earbud, responding to my sincere and maybe slightly hopeful skepticism about the oracle's accuracy this one time.

"If there's anyone in Thornsboro worth inspiring, I haven't met them yet," I grumbled.

"You just opened, Mason. Give it a chance. The Oracle sees that this is where you need to be. It's rare that she gives individual direction like this. Something important must be in store for you."

"Yeah? Well, I hope I wasn't sent to sling espresso in the boondocks of Northern Virginia for shits and giggles."

My late father was a member of the Zodiac Brotherhood, the defenders of our dragon race. He was a warrior. The bravest male I'd ever known. The Saint's Order killed him when I was still a boy. It had always been my dream to be a member of the brotherhood, to walk in the footsteps of Dad and my uncle Connor, but there are only twelve warrior dragons that defend our race, one for each celestial sign. I'm a Pisces, and a dragon named Solomon Chirag served in that position.

That didn't stop me from dreaming. I had warrior blood, which meant I was eligible to ascend to the position if something ever happened to Solomon.

Maybe someday.

"Trust. The stars are guiding you toward your destiny." Connor sounded so sure.

I pictured the hulking man on the other end of the line, who'd once carried me on his shoulders when I was a child, and wished I were in New York with him and the rest of my family.

"What if my destiny is to operate an espresso machine for the next thirty years?" I asked through a scowl.

"There are worse things." Connor's deep, gritty laugh held a tinge of compassion and a heaping spoonful of get-the-fuck-over-it.

The front bell chimed.

"Customer. Later, okay?" We said our goodbyes, and I

shoved my phone into my pocket. I strode from the back room to find a bundle of blond energy hurtling toward me with a hairy ball of filth in her arms. Her hair bounced behind her like her own cheering section, and the designer minidress she wore showed off legs that made me look twice.

"You!" Her large green eyes locked onto me and it was like being caught in a tractor beam. I was temporarily paralyzed by the intensity of her, as if a hurricane had set its eye on me. "Can you fetch us a dish of water please? It's an emergency."

And just like that, I was out of her spotlight. She sat herself at one of the tables and placed the furry thing near her feet. A small pink tongue emerged from the ball along with the sound of panting. A dog. A stray by the looks of things.

Mr. Pembrooke, the elderly man from across the street who'd been nursing an Americano for two hours, glanced in our direction. He folded his newspaper in a huff. "Reagan Bailey, you can't bring a dog into a restaurant! It's a health violation. That thing is full of fleas."

Reagan's head snapped around, and the look she shot Pembrooke made me lift an eyebrow. I would not want to be on the receiving end of that green fire. "That's bull-shit, Mr. P. First of all, this is an emergent situation. Someone abandoned this poor little dog on the side of the road, and I'm trying to get him help. Second, service dogs are allowed in restaurants and this is my brand-new emotional-support animal. So, if you don't like it, finish your coffee and go find Mrs. P. I'm sure she's missing your company."

The old man scowled as if the thought of spending time with his wife was downright repulsive, but he abandoned his paper, along with what was left of his coffee, and stomped out the door. I filled a bowl with water and brought it over, sliding it toward the black-haired mop. The tiny pink tongue set to work drinking greedily.

"Thank you," she said genuinely. "I'm sorry if I cost you a customer."

I snorted, still squatting beside the canine. "He's been nursing the same dollar coffee for hours. I think I'll survive."

She laughed, and it sounded like a bird singing. My inner dragon twisted inside me, waking up and heating my blood. Weird. Humans never had that effect on me. I stood and put space between us. Maybe she was a dragon? I inhaled deeply but smelled only vanilla, lavender, and dog.

"Hey, can I order a cappuccino? That is, if you don't mind my guest sticking around for a few more minutes. I should tell you he's not really a service animal." She slanted a playful smile, her hand still on the furball, and I thought my heart was going to crack my rib cage trying to get to her. Up close, Reagan Bailey was an enchantress with buttery-blond waves, curves that tested the buttons of her dress, and an arresting green-eyed stare that made my breath catch in my throat. *Fuck*, what was wrong with me? I wrangled myself under control and offered her a reassuring but professional smile.

"I had my suspicions." I winked, then glanced around the empty café. "I like animals. Make yourself comfortable. I'll get you that cappuccino."

Casually, I sauntered to the espresso machine, trying my best to brush off my strange reaction to the human. Even though dragons played a big part in the advancement of humanity, few knew about us. We lived secretly among man, our oldest, most sacred laws requiring our discretion with rare exceptions.

I didn't dislike humans—I simply considered them a different species and rarely thought of them at all aside from my role among them. But this one, Reagan—I wouldn't have minded if she were a dragon. She interested me.

After a few centering breaths, I lost myself in making her drink. For fun, I poured her foam in the shape of a dog's face. When I brought it out to her table, I cleared my throat to get her attention. She smiled bright enough to burn.

"Cute! Where'd you learn to do that?" She'd pulled Pembrooke's newspaper over to her table and absently toyed with the corner as she glanced between me and my creation.

"Washington State University. Majored in environmental science. Minored in espresso."

That elicited another laugh. I loved that laugh.

"I'm Reagan." She stuck out her hand. "Bailey."

Tentatively, I shook it, my inner dragon rumbling at the feel of her skin. I coughed to cover it up. "Mason. Forge."

"Oh, as in Forge's Café." She pointed at the door. "You own the place?"

I nodded.

"I have to tell you that the ambiance is about three thousand times better than old Mr. Baker's place. Don't tell anyone I said that. He was practically an institution in this town. Anyway, the important thing is the coffee. Let's see what you've got."

She picked up the mug and proceeded to drink and drink and drink until I was honestly curious how her mouth wasn't burning. She chugged it like a frat boy at a kegger. By the time she finally lowered the cup back to the saucer and wiped her lips with her thumb, my mouth was hanging open.

"Perfect. Only wish the mug was bigger."

"How are you not vibrating after drinking espresso like that?"

She flicked her hair over each shoulder. "Majored in journalism. Minored in coffee drinking." She tucked the paper under her arm. "Do you mind if I take this?"

I shook my head. "If Pembrooke comes back for it, I'll pretend I didn't see you help yourself."

"Thanks." She stood up, gathering the dog into her arms as if she planned to go. But then she stopped and gave me an inquisitive look. "If you were an environmental science major, how did you end up running a coffeehouse in Thornsboro?"

I shrugged. "I guess you could say it was meant to be."

She nodded appreciatively, then headed for the door.

"Why journalism?" I called after her.

Smiling over her shoulder, she said, "Because I'm going to save the world."

The door swung closed behind her. I pulled out my phone and texted Connor. *You were right. The Oracle always knows.*

Chapter Two

REAGAN

"Holy shit, have you seen the barista at that new café in town? The spot where Baker's used to be." I tapped the icon to put my best friend and coworker, Imani, on speakerphone, keeping one eye on the road as I drove home.

"Not yet. Didn't that place just open? Forge's, right?"

"Yeah, but trust me on this one, you need to get over there. The coffee is good, but the ambience is better. Six foot four, dark and dangerous, tower of muscle ambience."

"I'm suddenly craving a latte." She squealed.

The little black dog in the seat beside me perked his ears and barked at the high-pitched noise.

"Do you have a dog in the car with you, Reagan?" Imani asked, laughing.

"I found him on the side of the road. I think someone

dumped him. He's in bad shape, so I'm taking him home."

"I'm sure *Richard* is going to love that." Richard was my dad, otherwise known as Richard Bailey, CEO of Bailey Enterprises, the company behind the nationwide chain of Bailey Grocery stores. At one time we'd been close, but lately it was safe to say we'd developed a strained relationship. The details around what had sharpened the wedge between us were... complicated.

"Dad probably won't notice. The company is bidding on some new government contract. I don't know the details, but he works late every night and leaves early in the morning. I'm willing to bet that by the time my dad notices Pulitzer's there, he'll either be a member of the family or I will have found his rightful owner. I'll post a notice in the Thornsboro lost pets groups tonight on social."

"Pulitzer, huh?"

"Litz for short. I like that name, especially considering I think I'm onto something."

"Do tell."

"Remember how we noticed that Senator Cromwell was wearing that weird ring during his interview with CNN last Monday?" It wasn't something most people would notice. His hand only appeared in the frame for a fraction of a minute, but the Saint George cross etched into the face of the platinum ring caught my attention. It was an odd thing for a senator of the United States to wear. And when I enlarged the picture and read the inscription, it got even weirder.

"Yeah, it reminded you of the Skull and Bones rings the Yale society members wear."

"Right. Like it was homemade or something. Not what you usually see on someone of his stature, right?"

"Right."

"Well, I came across a picture in the *Washington Post* of Supreme Court Justice Maurice Shiller. Same ring."

"Jesus, Reagan. Do you think they're both members of a secret society?" Imani's voice rose with intrigue.

"I do, and based on their political ties, I think this group is extremely interested in maintaining the wealth and power of its members. Cromwell and Shiller have been pushing that bill that would make it harder for new competitors to enter the market."

"The Anderson bill."

"Right. They want people to think it's protecting jobs, but it's really hampering competition and innovation. Anyway, I'm going to do an image search tonight and see who else might be sporting this ring."

"This could be big, Reagan. If a secret society is pulling strings in Washington, breaking a story like that would definitely make waves. I'll do some digging too. I've got friends in dark places."

I laughed. Imani was a genius when it came to technology, and I had no doubt she'd be diving deep into the dark web tonight, looking for clues about the rings. "Thanks, lady. See you tomorrow."

"Love ya, woman."

"Always."

Imani and I have been friends since third grade and

have shared a love for investigative reporting for almost as long, although unlike me, whose focus is writing, the tools of her trade are camera and video. Unfortunately, coming from a tiny town in Virginia had severely limited our opportunities. We both worked for a small, rural newspaper called the *Independent*, where I'd taken an internship after graduating in May. My actual role was to write obituaries and the occasional community-news fluff piece, but my goal was to be promoted to investigative reporter by the time my yearlong internship was over. Breaking a story like this would be just the thing to secure the promotion.

I reached the Bailey Estate, passed through the gate, and drove the long, serpentine drive to my father's house. I'd lived there my entire life, but it didn't feel like my place. Three words came to mind as I pulled up to the door: *enormous*, *pretentious*, and *superfluous*. The damn house had ten rooms and fifteen bathrooms, and it was only my father and me living there. It was another way that this acorn had rolled far from the tree. Dad liked nice things. I preferred the simple life. Give me a strong coffee and a sweet pup like the one in the seat next to me and I had enough.

I parked in the circle and climbed out of my faded red Jetta, gathering the dog into my arms. "Come on Litz. Let's get you a bath and something to eat. Jesus, maybe a haircut too. I can't even see your eyes."

"Good evening, Ms. Reagan," our housekeeper Carlotta said from the door. "Mr. Bailey asked me to send you to his office the minute you got home. He needs to speak with you." Her eyes locked on my furry cargo. "Is that a dog?"

I flashed her a winsome smile. "Carlotta... is there any way you could watch Litz until I'm done speaking with my father? I need time to get Dad used to the idea."

She made the gimme gesture with her red-tipped fingers. "Hand him over."

I passed her the mutt and pecked her cheek. "You are the absolute best."

One of those red nails pointed in my direction. "And you are going to fall on your sword if I get in trouble for having this dog."

"Done. You were just following orders."

I patted her shoulder and crossed the marble foyer to the right side of the imperial staircase. My footsteps echoed in the high-ceilinged room, and I was relieved to reach the quiet comfort of the carpeted upstairs hallway. I knocked on my father's home office door.

"Come in."

Dad's office always reminded me of an old-world library, maybe one that belonged in a medieval castle. It was furnished in dark wood and lined with leather volumes of law and reference books and a few classics like *The Prince* by Machiavelli, which happened to be his personal favorite. My father sat behind a desk that could serve as a bomb shelter, his eyes fixed on a glowing monitor as he typed furiously, still wrapped up in a constricting gray suit. He used to be blond, but now his hair was mostly gray, which made his dark blue eyes appear twice as stark in the pale wash of his face.

"Ah, Reagan. Sit down. There's something I need to discuss with you."

I sat, automatically smoothing my hands over my jeans. Dad and I weren't in the habit of having personal heart-to-hearts. Those had disappeared soon after my mother died. It was sad really. All we had was each other. But after Mom's death, Dad had hidden in his work as if dollar bills and contracts contained an antidote for grief. He rarely came out from under them unless there were copious amounts of alcohol involved.

"Bailey Enterprises is gunning for a government contract to supply the state school-lunch program. We've got a good shot this year, Reag. We've scaled our institutional business, and we're positioned to grow exponentially."

"You mentioned something about that when you explained why you were working late. Congratulations. That's exciting." I rubbed my hands on my thighs, wishing we were at the kitchen table and not in this office. It felt too much like an interview. Too formal.

The smile he gave me shone like he was about to sell me a multilevel-marketing product. I braced myself.

"It is exciting, and it's time you were a part of it." *Oh shit.* "You're twenty-three years old. This is your family business, and this kind of growth means we need more help at the helm. We need a leader like you."

I shook my head, my words coming out choppy as I stated the obvious. "But I don't work for Bailey, Dad. I'm a journalist. I have an internship at the *Independent*."

He smiled wider. "Come on. We both know you're too

smart for the *Independent*. What I'm offering you is a real challenge, the chance to be part of something huge, an opportunity most people your age will never see in their lifetimes." Dad's voice became slightly strained, and his salesman smile faltered.

I wasn't giving him the reaction he wanted, but this line of conversation was coming out of left field. He'd had four years to get used to the idea of my becoming a journalist as a pursued my degree. He'd watched me walk across the stage and accept my diploma almost eight months ago. And while he hadn't exactly been excited about my taking an internship that paid minimum wage, he hadn't tried to stop me either.

I chewed my lip. "I appreciate you thinking of me. I do. But I *have* a job. I'm a journalist," I answered softly. "And I know the pay isn't what I'd be making if I worked for Bailey, but I'm driving distance from Washington, DC, a jackpot of investigative reporting opportunity. My year is almost up, and then I'll have enough experience to secure a real position somewhere with a livable salary. With any luck, it will be sooner."

His smile faded entirely, and the first lines of anger wrinkled the corners of his eyes. "You can't possibly think that writing obituaries and fluff pieces for a has-been paper with a meager circulation is a real job. Christ, you made more working the grocery checkout lane in high school."

"Only because you owned the store." I sighed. Dad was loaded. Like Scrooge McDuck swan diving into a pile of gold loaded. It was impossible for him to respect what I did because the value he placed on everything in his life revolved around the price tag attached to it. "The money doesn't matter to me. Being a journalist means something to me."

"Be serious." He ran a hand through his hair. "The only reason you think money isn't important is because you've always had it."

"I can make money doing what I love."

His face reddened and he gripped the side of his desk. "It's time you grew up and got your head out of the clouds!"

"How is being a reporter having my head in the clouds?" Agitated, I gathered my long blond hair into a ponytail behind my head and then pulled it all over one shoulder when I realized I didn't have an elastic. I twisted a strand around my finger, desperately wanting this conversation to end.

"For God's sake, that paper could go under at any moment and you'd have no job at all. This choice you made to *follow your dreams*—" He said it in a tone that made it clear he had no respect for the road I'd traveled. "It's romantic. But what I'm offering you is guaranteed. It means lifelong security!"

"I know you think that working for Bailey is what's best for me, but I wouldn't be happy there. Reporting is what I love. It's what I want to do."

He held up his hands in exasperation. "It's not a job, Reagan. It's charity."

"Only for a few more months, and then it will be more."

"You hope."

I tucked my hair behind my ears and gave it to him straight. "Look, it doesn't matter, because I have no interest in working for Bailey. I understand you want me to. You have for a while. But I can't do it. I want to report on stories that change the world. I want to be part of exposing injustice."

Dad ran a thumb along one brow, his lips pressing together in a pronounced frown. "It's not just about the job, Peanut. I was hoping if we worked together, we could be close again. Close like we used to be."

Uh-oh. He'd pulled out the childhood nickname. This was serious. "I want us to be close again too, but I don't have to work at Bailey for that to happen."

Dad pointed a finger my way. "You only say that because you're young and you've never had to fend for yourself. A few years struggling to make ends meet and you'd realize what a gift I'm offering you. Do you know how many kids would kill for an opportunity like this?"

I took a deep breath and blew it out slowly. "Then you should definitely interview them because your daughter isn't interested."

"Take some time and think about it." A muscle in his jaw twitched. The look he gave me made his words sound like an ultimatum.

My blood frosted in my veins. "And if I think about it and my choice is to stay at the paper?"

His eyes shifted toward his monitor. "I sincerely hope I've raised you to make better choices. If I haven't, I'll need to give you a lesson in reality. Things will have to change."

"Change how?"

"Let's cross that bridge when we come to it."

He didn't have to say more. Either I went to work for him or there would be consequences. And if I had to guess what those consequences would involve, I'd guess I wouldn't have a room here anymore.

"Mom would want me to follow my dreams," I mumbled.

"Your mother isn't here, Peanut. What she would or wouldn't want is moot. This is how it is and how it has to be." He pointed a knuckle at me. "I'm doing this because I love you and I know I'm right. This company, it's your legacy, and I'm not going to make it easy for you to throw it away. Not without a fight. Think about my offer. Take a few weeks to get used to the idea. We'll talk again soon."

Inside, my stomach twisted. A couple more weeks wouldn't change my mind. I had no intention of working for my father. Not ever. And the one thing I knew for sure about Dad was he didn't take no for an answer. As long as I was under his roof, he'd expect me to comply with his wishes.

Which meant I couldn't be under his roof anymore. I nodded once, rose from my seat, and strode from his office, knowing that in just a few weeks, I'd need to have a place to live and a means to support myself. And as I jogged down the steps to find Carlotta, I remembered there was someone else I needed to worry about now. *Litz.*

Fuck my life.

Chapter Three

MASON

I saw Reagan again the very next day. She chose the table near the window. I remember feeling happy that she grabbed it before Pembroke crossed the street and camped there for the day. There were a few other people in the place: a woman passing through town on her way to Heritage Grove, and the owner of the local hardware store, Mr. Whitman. Most of the time, people came to the counter to order, but I couldn't stop my feet from carrying me to her table the moment she sat down.

"You're back," I said, inhaling deeply to pick up that vanilla and lavender scent of hers. She smelled like a candle, the homey kind evocative of fresh-baked cookies.

"Oh, hi Mason." She beamed up at me with that megawatt smile of hers. "Yeah, you should know that now that I've tasted your coffee, I will be a regular fixture here. You're saving me a thirty-minute drive to the nearest Starbucks."

My inner dragon purred, and I set my hands on my hips to just stare at her. After much too long, I noticed her smile fade and realized that I wasn't blinking. Creator, I probably came across like some sort of freak. I cleared my throat. "What can I get for you?"

She laughed and shook her head a little, a blush staining her creamy skin as if she was the awkward one for not knowing what I was waiting for. "A cappuccino, please. The biggest one you've got."

"Right. Okay." Reluctantly, I left her to prepare her drink. Technically, I only had one size cappuccino on the menu, and it was made with two shots of espresso, but I grabbed a latte mug and threw in three shots. Then I poured her foam in the shape of a dog's face again.

When I brought it over to her table, she had her laptop open and was typing furiously, but paused what she was working on to offer me a smile. "Oh! It looks just like Litz!"

"Litz?"

"The little dog who I brought in here before. I named him Pulitzer, Litz for short."

"So, uh, he didn't already have a name then?"

"No," she said emphatically. "I posted his picture in all the Thornsboro lost pet groups and the free paper. No one has claimed him. You know, I think someone dumped him on purpose."

"And you plan to give him a home, if he doesn't already have one."

She smiled and brushed her bright blonde curls from her shoulder. Honestly, she must have been a witch or something, the way her hair held the light. God, when she looked at me with those green eyes of hers, it was like seeing a sunrise. "Of course, silly. What else would I do with him?"

I shrugged. "Some people would take a found dog to the humane society... or the pound. Some people might leave it where they found it."

She gasped as if the notion positively appalled her. "Some people need to have their heads examined. The dog distribution system tapped me on the shoulder, Mason, and I won't be turning away the free gift. Besides, if you could see him now that I've bathed and groomed him, you wouldn't even recognize him. He belongs in a dog show. Whoever dumped him didn't know what they had."

For a moment, I was stunned by my jealousy of this dog, Litz. To be loved like that, after only a day. Warm, unconditional love. Reagan simply decided that fate had sent her a dog, and that was that, with no expectation of anything in return. She was as kind and warmhearted as she was beautiful. *Fuck, how was she real?*

"Do you have a dog?" she asked.

"No," I said honestly, but when I registered disappointment on her face, I amended my answer. "I want one, though. I'm quite fond of my uncle Connor's German Shepherd, Bones. It's just, I am renting a cottage from the Wilsons and pets aren't allowed. Someday though."

"Right," she said, her smile fading as if something I'd said had triggered her. "Have you moved around a lot since Washington State?"

"I spent a couple years in Maine, working in a National Forrest."

"And then you came here... to Thornsboro... to open a coffee shop?"

"I like it here." The corner of my mouth twitched. I loved the way she looked at me when she was trying to figure me out. My smile grew a little fuller. I was a riddle she'd never solve. Dragons did not reveal themselves to humans. But it was fun to watch her try. Fun and maybe an exquisite torture. For some reason, I wanted her to figure it out. I wanted her to know me.

"Well, thank you for this." She raised her cappuccino and turned back to her computer.

I excused myself by mumbling something about getting back to work and scrambled for the privacy of the kitchen. Really, I just wanted to catch my runaway heart and force it back into the cage of my chest. Creator, help me. *A human*. I needed to get a grip.

Chapter Four

REAGAN

That week, I turned up the steam on investigating my probable secret society. I needed to turn this theory into a paycheck before my father's foot came down. As it was, I sensed it hovering over my head like I was a spider who had just found itself in a shoe-shaped shadow. Before work, I asked Imani to meet me for coffee at Forge's. I wanted to share what I'd learned and see if she had any ideas about next steps. I also wanted to see Mason.

The handsome barista has garnered more of my attention than I wanted to admit. There was just something about him. When he brought Litz the dish of water the first day we met, he had such warmth in his eyes. He wasn't worried about dirt or flees or the fact that I completely lied about him being a service dog. He was just a big man giving a tiny dog a drink. Every time I thought about it my heart melted like ice cream on the fourth of July.

"So, how's the exposé coming?" Imani asked. We were still in the parking lot, and she looked far too sophisticated for Thornsboro in a sharp yellow blazer with her long braids wound around the crown of her head.

"Every person we've seen pictured wearing the ring, I've followed like a stalker on social. Not just the major outlets, the minor ones too. But these people are careful about their public personas. I've noticed they often try to hide the ring as well. What I'm doing now is following their wives, their children, the people who they take pictures with at events."

Imani nodded approvingly as she swung open the door to Forge's. "From what you've found, are the members are all men?"

"Every one. And no one without a B as in billion after their net worth. This society is composed exclusively of rich, powerful men. Not an Oprah or Taylor in the bunch."

"Interesting. What do you need me to do?"

My gaze immediately shot around the cafe, looking for Mason, but he must have been in the back because I didn't find him anywhere. Noone was behind the counter. Pembrook was by the window, so I pulled out a chair at a four top near the fireplace. Imani sat down across from me. "Can you use your special skills to get me connections on any of the anonymous or easily disguisable forums? Discord, Reddit, etc." I handed her the folder containing a list of family and friends of our suspects. "I want personal accounts. Anything where someone might slip up and talk about Fight Club."

She snorted. "Happy to."

She leaned over to put the folder away in her bag, but paused when Mason appeared beside our table out of nowhere.

"Oh, hello," I said in soft surprise.

He slid a red cup the size of a soup bowl in front of me—a cappuccino, with the foam poured to look like a sleeping kitten. The darling critter was so lifelike, I was afraid our voices would wake it, and it would lift its head and open its foam eyes.

"I took a chance. Cappuccino right? The biggest one I've got?" He slanted a crooked, panty-melting grin in my direction.

"Yes," I said breathlessly. "It's perfect. Even bigger than last time." I looked around and to the rack behind the counter. All his mugs were white with a gold band around the collar— except this one. "Is this a new mug."

He laughed, low and throaty. "I got it for you. Found it in Heritage Grove."

Our eyes met and held. "That's forty-five minutes from here."

"You're a very good customer," he said softly, soft like we were lying in bed and he'd whispered it to me from the other side of the pillow we were sharing.

I forgot to breathe. I forgot where I was. Until a perfectly manicured black hand slowly extended between us.

"Hi, I'm Imani."

We both snapped out of the trance we were in. I cleared my throat. "Yes! Oh my gosh. This is my friend, Imani. Imani, this is Mason. He owns Forge's. I think I told you about coming in here with Litz the other day." I turned toward her and tugged on my earlobe to ground myself. *Jesus, what had just happened?*

"Very nice to finally meet you," Imani said smoothly, taking her time shaking his hand.

"What can I get for you?" Mason asked her. "I only have the one red mug but if you are a volume cappuccino drinker like Reagan, I can bring you two if you'd like." He flashed her a disarming smile.

Imani was never the type to be overly impressed with any man, but I noticed her lashes flutter a few times before she answered. "Actually a chai is more my speed. Regular size. Thank you."

Mason nodded and took off for the counter. I sipped my cappuccino, closing my eyes when dark silk hit my tongue. Mmm.

"Holy shit," Imani whispered. "Are you sleeping with Mason the barista?"

I swallowed quickly because there was no way I was wasting that drink by blowing it all over her. "No!"

Her eyes widened. "Why the fuck not?"

I laughed. "I know, right? He's like... magnetic or something."

She arched a brow. "The chemistry between you two is giving nuclear vibes."

I sigh. "I ... I barely know him really. Just from coming in here since he opened."

"But you're interested."

I snorted. "Who wouldn't be?"

Mason returned with Imani's drink but kept his eyes on me as he slid the cup in front of her. It was so obvious, she gave me a conspiratorial grin.

"Looks like you two are hard at work," he said, his eyes falling on the folder sticking out of Imani's bag. "I'll leave you to it."

"Your girl, Reagan, is on the verge of cracking a tremendous story," Imani blurted before he could walk away.

He stopped and faced me, lighting up like someone just plugged him in. "Not at all surprised. First day I met her she said she was going to change the world." He winked at me, and my pulse skipped a beat. "What is this groundbreaking story about?"

"I'm sorry, but that's classified." I told him. "It's super-secret."

His dark brow arched. "You could tell me but then you'd have to kill me?"

"Exactly."

"All right. I see how it is."

"No offense." I took another long drink of my coffee.

"None taken." Loud tapping on the windows interrupted us. A storm had moved in, and hail thundered against the glass. Even Pembrook took a break from his morning paper to frown at the assault, as if he was worried the ice might break through.

"Careful out there this morning," Mason said. "Looks like we're in for a bad storm."

"I hate storms," I murmured, although hate didn't exactly cover how I felt about them.

Imani squeezed my hand supportively.

Mason rubbed the side of his face. "You hate the rain?"

"My mother passed away during a big storm," I said. "Sometimes the thunder wakes the grief monster."

He frowned, his eyes catching on the way Imani held my hand. "I'm familiar with that particular beast," he said, then immediately tagged on. "You're welcome to stay until it stops. Or I can grab an umbrella and walk you to your car."

"We're big girls. We'll be fine," Imani said.

She was right to refuse. I was thankful for the gesture, but he had a business to run.

His eyes drifted over me one more time, and then he just nodded and headed for the counter.

"Jesus, Mary, and Joseph," Imani said once he was gone. "Girl, you gonna have to start ordering ice coffee, because this right here—" She waved a fingernail between me and the direction Mason went. "—about ready to burst into flames. Pure fire, my friend."

We finished our drinks then ran to our cars in the pouring rain, me regretting not taking Mason up on the offer to walk me to my car.

Chapter Five

MASON

Humans don't make good mates. I reminded myself often of that fact every time Reagan came into Forge's Café. And she was there a lot. Sometimes, it felt like I was going through the motions each day until she walked through the front door, bubbling over with stories of how Litz had stolen her socks or how Imani had kept her up too late watching the latest's thriller on her streaming service.

Something about her always managed to pull me in. I had the sense I was here for her, that I was supposed to inspire her in a way that mattered. A dragon's presence among humans was enough to ignite creative magic within them. I didn't know exactly how my presence was affecting her, but all the signs confirmed it was. She visited every day, working feverishly on her laptop, sometimes accompanied by her friend Imani. And no matter how busy I was, I always ended up lingering at her table.

Today, I slid her cappuccino in front of her and waited for her reaction. I'd poured the foam to look like two koi fish swimming yin-yang in that special, over-sized red cup I'd started using just for her. Had I intentionally re-created the Pisces symbol, my zodiac dragon sun sign, in her cappuccino? Yes. Yes I had. And I'd served it up in that mug I'd driven forty-five minutes to procure especially for her. I didn't break out the red mug for any other customer. I tried not to analyze all the ways I favored Reagan. It wasn't part of my role as a dragon to dote on her like I did. I simply couldn't help myself.

"Oh my god, Mason." She smiled up at me from her seat, her green eyes twinkling. "It's beautiful. And you used my favorite cup again! You're the best." I had to consciously and purposefully stop myself from returning a derpy grin.

"Need fuel for that supersecret project of yours." I gestured at the pile of papers in front of her.

"I appreciate that. But this is not the secret project. This is me trying to find an apartment."

"You're moving out of your old place?"

She shrugged. "Yeah. I currently live with my dad, and it's time I stood on my own two feet."

"Any prospects?"

"One or two places." She sipped her cappuccino, her eyes darting away like it was a touchy subject.

I drummed my fingers on the back of the chair across the table from her, curious as hell and wondering how far I should probe. "About that secret project, are you ever going to tell me what you're working on?"

Her brow arched. "Are you ever going to tell me why someone who went to school in Vancouver and worked for years in Maine ended up slinging coffee in Thornsboro?"

I laughed. "We've been over this. I came here on a whim."

"Yeah," she drawled. "It's not adding up for me."

"So... the secret project?"

"Not yet. I'll tell you when I've put more of the pieces together."

The café had cleared out, so I took a seat across from her. "Tell me this then. The first day you were in here, you said you wanted to save the world. What did you mean by that?" I'd always wondered what made her choose those words and had a suspicion I could guess what her project was by her answer.

"Martin Luther King said that darkness can't drive out darkness. Only light can do that. Light comes from knowing the truth, and journalism, at least for me, is about finding and broadcasting the truth."

I groaned. "Is it though? I feel like there are versions of the truth, and everyone has one."

"That's a bit cynical." She laughed. "I believe when people know better, they do better."

Gods, I loved her exuberance. "Maybe."

"You must believe that people are generally good or you wouldn't own this place."

"I don't follow." I leaned forward, studying her.

"You've devoted your life to making people happy, one cup of coffee at a time." She lifted her mug and took a long sip. Her eyes closed, and she moaned softly at the taste. The sound made me squirm in my chair.

I cleared the thickness from my throat and took a tight hold of my inner dragon. "Tell me how your coffee addiction started. Was there a gateway drug? Tea? Hot cocoa?"

She giggled. "No. I used to run track in high school. Seven a.m. practices. I was hooked from my first cup. That wasn't a cappuccino, though. It was whatever my dad was drinking. I never know with him. Could have been Folger's or could have been some priceless imported blend. I wouldn't have known the difference back then."

"A runner, huh? I would've pegged you for a cheerleader." I caught myself leaning across the table, breathing in her scent. Shit, I was sniffing her like she was a flower. Her eyes narrowed on my nose, then on my mouth. She knew I'd just smelled her. She totally knew. I leaned back in my chair and tried to act casual while my inner dragon chuffed for me to touch her, see if she felt as good as she smelled.

"Couldn't cut it as a cheerleader. I liked the outfits, but I wasn't coordinated enough to do the cheers."

I blinked, trying not to picture her in a short skirt. I

failed miserably. She had great legs. In a tiny skirt like cheerleaders wore, one that barely covering her ass? My imagination ran wild.

"How about you? Did you play sports?"

I chuckled. It probably wasn't fair that dragons played against humans, but because we lived with them, it was almost unavoidable. "Lacrosse and soccer, but what I really love is rock climbing."

"An outdoor enthusiast." She sipped her coffee. "I love that for you."

"You're not a fan of the great outdoors?"

Her smile faded. "Not anymore. My mom used to take me camping when I was small, but after she died, we never went again. Honestly, I'm not sure if I'd like it or not now."

"I'm sorry... about your mom."

"It was a long time ago. She died when I was eleven of a congenital heart defect."

Reagan toyed with her mug, and I chided myself for bringing up a terrible memory. But worse, we had this in common, and before I could stop myself, I blurted. "My father died when I was young as well." At least I'd kept the fact that he was murdered to myself. Gods, how did you bring a conversation back from that? I drummed my fingers on the table, then rose from my chair when things between us turned introspective. "I should get back to work."

"Wait!" She caught my wrist, and when she touched me, a current of electricity flowed up my arm. She had my full attention. I couldn't have moved if I tried. "Would you like to have a real date sometime? We seem to get along pretty well, and, uh, I'd like to see you." Her brow furrowed. "Maybe we could skip talking about our childhood traumas and go straight to our opinions on cat videos. Dinner?"

I swallowed. Fuck, I wanted to say yes. The problem was, I genuinely liked her. Worse, my dragon was extremely interested. But if my father's death had taught me anything, it was that liking someone too much was a mistake. Liking someone might lead to love, and love was a dangerous sport to play. People, especially fragile humans, tended to die if you loved them too much. And I was a dragon. Any relationship between us would be... complicated to say the least.

I looked down at the table. "I'm sorry... I can't. It's not you. I'm just..." I exhaled through my nose and looked her in the eye. "I'm not in a place to date right now." God, that sounded like a cop-out.

Her face fell and her hand drifted from my wrist, leaving me cold. "I understand." She glanced at her empty mug. "I didn't just make it weird for me to come in here, did I? Because I really like your coffee and think of you as a friend."

Smiling, I shook my head. "Not weird at all. And we are... friends."

"Cool." She stood and packed up her things. "Later, *friend*."

I watched her walk out the door, feeling like a finalist in the biggest-idiot awards. The last thing I wanted was to be her friend. She was the best part of my day and the only good thing about living in Thornsboro. I ran a heavy hand down my face. No, I'd done the right thing. No good could come from dating a human. I returned to work, my inner dragon grumbling in misery.

Chapter Six

REAGAN

"Please, God, send an earthquake to open a crevice large enough to swallow me whole so that I never have to face Mason Forge again." I groaned as I headed for home with Imani on speakerphone.

"Uh-oh. What happened?"

"I asked him on a date and he turned me down."

"Huh? Why? You two have been flirting like horny teenagers for weeks. Honestly, I'm surprised he hasn't made a move before this."

"Thank you! I mean, what the hell, right?"

"Right."

For a few minutes I just stared at the road, fuming. "I need sex, Imani."

"I can't help you with that," she said flatly.

"It's been a dry spell. A drought. A cracked-earth dust bowl era of physical intimacy."

"Have you tried Tinder?"

"It's not that I haven't had opportunity. My vagina doesn't want anyone but him. It's like there's this magnetic draw between us. Every time I'm in there, my panties are on fire. I mean, thank fuck he runs a coffee shop and not an ice-cream parlor or the freezer wouldn't be able to keep up."

"Go home. Have some of that ice cream you mentioned and cool off."

"I'm going to need a bucket of ice cream. Maybe a bathtub of ice cream. And honestly, I could have sworn he felt it, too."

"Maybe it's not you, it's him? He has a mysterious past. You told me he said he opened Forge's here on a whim. That's totally sus."

My eyes narrowed. "True." Suddenly, an idea came to me and I gasped. "What if the reason he can't date me is that he's in the witness-protection program and is super secretive because he's hiding from the mob?"

Imani hmmmed approvingly. "It's a good theory. He could also be a burn victim who's really embarrassed by his scars. Or have a micropenis."

"Yeah, yeah. That's totally possible. He's pushing me away because he's embarrassed about his body. I'm starting to feel much better about this."

"How's the apartment search going?"

"There's a place over Whitman's Hardware that I might be able to afford, but Mr. Whitman says no pets. I'm still negotiating because it's basically an attic and I doubt he has a long line of potential renters lined up for the place, but I'm not sure what I'll do with Litz if I can't change his mind."

Imani groaned. "Your dad won't reconsider, huh?"

"Strictly speaking, it's not him forcing me to move out."

"What? I thought he gave you an ultimatum?"

"Not in so many words. Since my mom died, all we've had is each other, but my father is obsessed with Bailey Enterprises. He wants to involve me in the business, but I know it's not for me. Only every time I tell him no, it's like I'm disappointing him all over again. I've come to realize that he'll never see me as my own person or accept that I'm never coming to work for the company unless I move out. And frankly, it's just a matter of time before he gives me the boot, anyway."

"God, I'm sorry, Reagan." Imani sighed into the phone. "If it will help, I can take Litz temporarily until you're back on your feet."

"I may have to take you up on that offer. You know what would really help my situation?"

"What?"

"You telling me you found something out about those rings."

"It's your lucky day. I've got great news."

"Hit me with it," I said excitedly.

"I've been investigating the names you sent me, everyone you've found with that ring."

A tingle traveled over my scalp. "Oh my god, what?"

"Some emails from the 1980s on the dark web. They were images of emails actually... scans that were never cleaned up from some data migration. That's probably why they persisted. They weren't named or tagged with anything but gibberish. Makes them hard to find to eliminate."

"How did you find them?"

"By investigating their source. I intentionally mined 'garbage' that fell off the truck, so to speak, during government system upgrades. Systems analysts are notoriously sloppy with this kind of work. Anyway, these emails contained a reference to a group called the Saint's Order."

"The Saint's Order," I repeated. "Creepy. Almost sounds like a religious sect."

"I know, right? This email mentions meeting at a member's home. It's vague, but it's something."

"Send it to me. I've got seventy-two names so far of people in influential positions who've been photographed wearing the ring. Now we have the name of their secret society."

"What's next?" she asked.

I thought for a second. "I'm going to follow the social media accounts of every known member like I have nothing else to do with my life. If they fart and social hears it, I'll know." "Excellent. Let me know what you find out."

"Will do." I parked in the garage and said goodbye, tossing my laptop bag over my shoulder and typing my key code into the lock to open the door to the mudroom. Litz met me, turning excited circles and whimpering for me to pick him up. I kicked off my shoes and hung up my coat before swooping him into my arms and kissing him on his black button nose.

After I'd bathed him and trimmed his hair, he turned out to be quite the handsome dog. I was guessing a shih tzu mix by his overall size and the shape of his tail. He'd taken to potty training like a champ too. His only bad habit was stealing my dirty socks and hiding them under my bed at night.

Carlotta appeared in the door to the mudroom, looking grim. "Ooooh, Ms. Reagan, your father came home early today. He's asked to see you the moment you arrive home. He saw the dog too. You know how Litz likes to follow me around while I vacuum. I'm so sorry."

I waved a hand dismissively. "It was absolutely not your responsibility to keep Litz a secret, Carlotta. The fact that he's lived here all this time without my father knowing is a pretty good indicator of how much Dad really cares if he's here. I'll talk to him. It'll be fine. He's all bark and no bite."

She shook her head. "I'm not so sure about that this time, Reagan. He's changed. This project—he's always on edge. He screamed at Rio yesterday for the state of the flowers around the pool. It's February! He can't keep flowers alive in this weather, and neither of you are using the pool anyway."

That was upsetting. Rio was the sweetest groundskeeper ever. He didn't deserve being yelled at or saddled with unrealistic expectations. "I'll try to talk to him, okay? He shouldn't be snapping at you or Rio."

"Thank you. He's lucky to have you as his daughter. You're a good person."

I gave her a quick hug and then headed for the stairs with Litz still in my arms. But as I approached Dad's office, I heard him yelling and slowed my footsteps on the carpet.

"We can't afford to lose this. This is our time. Make it happen!"

Through the door, I heard a thunk like he'd tossed his cell phone onto his desk. After a moment or two of silence, I set Litz down outside the door, knocked twice, and let myself in. His back was to me with his hands on his hips, flaring out the corners of his suit jacket. He stared out the window overlooking the backyard as if he didn't even hear me come in.

"Dad?" I prompted softly.

He whirled and it was like no time had passed since the last time I was in this room. "I need your answer, Reagan," he barked, slicing a pointed finger through the air at me. "Are you coming on board or not?"

I thought about lying or couching my words to soften the blow. It would be so easy to say I was still thinking about it. But I wasn't a liar, and I respected Dad too much to play games. "My answer is no, Dad. I've found my passion, and it's not with Bailey. I'm sorry."

He pitched forward to catch himself on the desk, his chest heaving. "Are you sure I can't change your mind?"

"Positive."

"You have two weeks."

"Two weeks until what?" I knew what, but I needed him to say it.

"You and that dog have two weeks to get out. You can't live here anymore, Reagan. I won't enable this pipe dream you've been living any longer." His voice was raised, and my stomach clenched at the fury in it. "Unless you come to your senses and change your mind."

Tears welled in my eyes. I'd seen this coming, but it hurt anyway. "I've already made arrangements. I'll be out by the end of next week." I had just enough time to register genuine surprise on Dad's face before I rushed from his office and straight to my room, anxious to retrieve my laptop from my bag. I needed to throw back the curtain on the Saint's Order, and fast. Breaking a story of this magnitude was my only hope of becoming a self-supporting adult.

And suddenly that was my top priority.

THREE DAYS LATER, I HAD IT. I MARCHED INTO MY EDITOR'S office, a stack of folders in my hands. "Mr. Patterson, do you have a minute?"

"Sure, have a seat. And call me Ed." He gestured at the chair across the desk, and I closed the door before taking a seat.

Patterson had always struck me as a man who was conventionally attractive when he was younger. Tall and fit, he still had a full head of hair, although it was grayer than brown these days and the skin under his eyes bagged like he hadn't slept since the Bush administration. Still, I'd always found him approachable, like his soul had maintained some fragment of his twentysomething self that I could relate to.

"I have a lead on a story. Technically, it's outside my scope of responsibilities, but—"

He held up a hand. "This internship is for your benefit, Reagan. It can be a platform to spring toward anything you want to reach. Show me what you've got."

I opened the folder and started walking him through how I'd put it all together. The list of names, the rings, the evidence that linked them all to the Saint's Order. Once I showed him the major clue I'd found on social, I knew I had him. There was an event happening next Friday within an hour's drive of Thornsboro, an event that promised to prove my hypothesis about the Saint's Order. I'd figured out where and when they were going to meet next. Having the names of a sizable number of members was key. Following their social media like a stalker and a few follow-up calls, and it'd all come together.

"It's good, Reagan. This is big. We'd definitely run this if you can make a direct connection between these names and the Order. Do you think you can get pictures or video of the event?"

I nodded. "Yes. I'll take Imani."

"Do it. I look forward to reading the finished piece." He pushed the folder toward me and started to turn back toward his computer, but I stayed exactly where I was. "Is there something else?"

"If I write this and you run the story, I want a position as an investigative reporter. Full salary and benefits."

He leaned back in his chair and threaded his fingers over his stomach. "Ah. You want to end your internship early and embark on the golden-handcuffs phase of adulthood."

I lifted my brows. "Huh?"

"Golden handcuffs. Once you're salaried, you're locked into a career. There's no escaping without taking a financial risk."

"I desperately need to wear the golden handcuffs, Ed."

He gave a low chuckle. "I'll have to clear it with HR, but if you pull off this story,

Reagan, I'll find a way to bring you onboard."

I blew out a deep breath and flattened a hand to my chest. "Thank you. Oh my god, thank you. I'm going to wow you with this piece."

He lifted an eyebrow. "I fully expect you will."

Chapter Seven

REAGAN

I was so close. A week from now, I'd have all the source material I needed to write a story that would change the trajectory of my life forever. And that wasn't all that was changing. I'd called Mr. Whitman after speaking with my editor. Not only did I have an appointment to sign a lease on his apartment next week, but he'd also said he'd make an exception for Litz. Everything was falling into place. Only one thing was missing.

Despite my embarrassment at his rejection, I couldn't wait to tell Mason. It was time to put our newly labeled friendship to the test, because until I shared this with him, none of it would feel real.

I shouldered open the door and allowed the cozy but sophisticated decor of Forge's Café to wash over me. Mason had done an incredible job remodeling the building. I couldn't remember the last time I was in Baker's, but I remember it was a pit. Now the place was decked out in natural fibers, green plants, and dark wood tables. A fire burned in an electric fireplace in the corner, surrounded by a blue velvet sofa and armchair. The bar was polished and the espresso machine behind it glinted in all its silver glory. Forge's could have succeeded in any major city. Again, I wondered what secrets Mason was hiding that had driven him here of all places.

It was unseasonably cold that day, even for February, and it took me a solid two minutes to strip out of my hat, gloves, and coat. Thankfully I was the only one there. I stuffed my cold weather clothes on the chair next to me and slid onto a stool at the bar.

Mason appeared from the back room and stopped abruptly when he saw me, his throat bobbing on a swallow. "Hi," he finally said.

"Hi," I echoed. "Fuck. This is awkward isn't it? I shouldn't have—"

"No!" he said quickly. "I just... You haven't been in for a few days. I wasn't sure what happened to you. I'm relieved to see you actually."

I smiled at that. "Oh good."

"Cappuccino?"

"Always." I grinned.

I answered a few emails, listening to the machine whir in the background. A few minutes later, he slid my drink toward me in my favorite oversized red mug. He'd poured the foam in the shape of a dragon, sprinkled with cinnamon along its spine. "My god, Mason, that is a work of art," I said before lifting my gaze. Our gazes locked and lashed like two sheets on a laundry line tangled in a storm. I swear I saw heat in his. I wondered if there wasn't something to the theories Imani and I had thrown out. Unless my radar was completely off, this man wanted me.

God, he was hot. Tonight, his dark hair curled out from the bottom of a beany, and he looked like he hadn't shaved today, giving him a healthy stubble that wasn't quite a beard. When he looked at me, his blue eyes reminded me of the week our family had spent in the Caribbean when my mom was still alive. Mason made my ovaries shiver every time I looked at him.

"Do you like dragons?" he asked, his voice low and smooth as silk. I wanted to close my eyes and have him read me the menu.

"Marry me," I blurted, chuckling a little. I'd meant it as a joke, but at the increase in intensity in Mason's eyes, I thought I'd better let him in on it. "Sorry. I was trying to be funny. Probably inappropriate given our last interaction. Um, I'm not crazy, just insanely thankful for this breathtaking hot espresso beverage. It's almost too beautiful to drink. Almost." I raised the cup to my lips and savored the silky heat that flowed down my throat. Mmmm.

His smile was back, and the crinkles at the corners of his eyes made a reappearance. "You didn't answer my question."

"About dragons? Who doesn't love dragons?" I took another sip.

His smile widened, and a glint of mischief entered his eyes. "You'd be surprised."

Was there anything sexier than a man secure enough in his masculinity to appreciate dragons? I bet he read fantasy novels.

"Who taught you to pour like this?" I ran through what I'd learned about Mason over the past weeks in my mind. He'd worked his way through college as a barista while majoring in environmental science, then took a job for the state of Maine as an environmental specialist before, for reasons—he said it was on a whim—he moved to Thornsboro and opened a café. I loved that he was an idealist when it came to the environment but that he also saw the value in making people happy with something as simple as coffee.

"My friend Andy. We used to have coffee-foam art competitions. The patrons would vote. I'd like to say mine always won, but she made a sleeping wolf that looked so real I thought it might howl."

I raised a brow. "So, uh, is Cat Foam Andy the reason you don't date?" I really should have dropped all this, but the journalist in me couldn't let it go.

"Cat Foam Andy is like a sister to me, and no, I don't date because..." He paused, searching my face.

"Because..."

He took a deep breath through his nose, those blue eyes as turbulent as a stormy sea. "I have a dark side, Reagan. There are things about me that would unsettle a potential partner. I just don't want to waste anyone's time."

I folded my arms. "But if you don't trust anyone with this potential dark side, you'll never have anyone in your life. Besides, some people like it dark." I lifted my coffee and sipped the dark espresso to drive the point home.

He leaned forward on his elbows, the hard lines of his face coming seductively close to mine. "If it were as easy as a cup of coffee, I'd already have shared it with you. Take my word for it, I'm dangerous."

Dangerous because he smelled as good as he looked, and all I wanted to do was close that few inches of space between us and find out if his lips were as soft as they seemed. I sighed. I reached out and took his hands between my own. "You know I'm a journalist, right? You can't tell me there's some mysterious reason you don't date and that you're dark and dangerous and then not explain why. Now I'm curious as hell. Are you in the witness-protection program?"

He pulled his hands away from mine like my touch had burned him, standing taller and crossing his arms. "No. But you have a vivid imagination."

We stared at each other like two gunfighters in a duel.

I heaved a beleaguered sigh. "Fine. I have something to tell you anyway."

"What?"

"My supersecret project is almost in the bag."

He laughed in that deep rumble that I could always feel at my center. "Congratulations."

"Well, I wanted you to know because every major breakthrough I've had investigating this story has come from right here. You may not realize it, but you're my muse." I'd never actually told Mason the specifics of what I'd been working on, but somehow something he did or said always helped me.. "It's one of the many reasons I come here, besides the great coffee and my friendship with the dark-and-dangerous barista."

Our eyes locked again, and the magnetic draw was back, stronger than before. I crossed my legs against a burgeoning ache between them. Mason backed away, frowning like I'd insulted him, something akin to shock registering on his face. He grabbed a bar towel and started vigorously wiping the counter.

Maybe that was too forward. Too flirty. What was wrong with me? I was like a guy who couldn't take no for an answer tonight.

"You're close to breaking your story then?" he asked through his teeth. Was that a bead of sweat on his temple?

Shit. I should stop pressing him before I embarrassed myself. But I couldn't help it. I couldn't let it go until I knew for sure why he wasn't interested in me. "I'll tell you all the juicy details," I promised, "if you tell me why you don't date."

Chapter Eight

MASON

Reagan had no idea the danger she was in. My inner dragon was very close to sprouting wings, leaping over the counter, and claiming her in the way of my kind. In the weeks I'd gotten to know her, I'd experienced attraction to her and then affection for her, but today, when I saw her standing in my café, my dragon wanted to mate her. Reagan was as stunning and perceptive as any dragon. But she *wasn't* a dragon. She was human. If that wasn't problematic enough, she was a journalist and painfully curious about everything. Exactly the wrong person to become involved with when you were harboring a dark secret.

Logically I knew that, but my body and the beast within it had different plans. When she'd touched me, mating sickness—my kind called it *appetency*—slammed into me like a million fluttering moths to a kindled flame.

My dragon wanted Reagan, he'd chosen her, and if he didn't have her soon, things were going to get uncomfortable fast.

"What's wrong? You look like you're going to be sick." She pressed her palm against my forehead, and I had to consciously stop myself from licking it. "Oh, you're warm. I think you might have a fever."

I jerked away as an electric current flowed directly from her touch to my dick. My stomach twisted and my balls tightened. *Fuck.* I reached for my phone. "What day is it today?"

"February nineteenth," she mumbled, nothing but concern in those green eyes and the turn of those pouty lips.

Dammit, I wanted to hoist her up on the counter, tear off her leggings, and fuck her into tomorrow. She licked her lips, and a fantasy of having that tongue on my cock left me blotting sweat from my brow.

"Yeah, you are definitely getting sick."

Yes, I was, with appetency. How had I lost track of the date? As a Pisces dragon, February nineteenth was the date I entered my alignment, the month of the year when the sun was in Pisces and thus my inner dragon was most tied into the celestial energy that ruled our kind. For the next month, I'd be at my most powerful but also experience my strongest urge for sex. In the past, it had been easy enough to get by with a visit to a few dragon females who were in the same physiological boat. But when Reagan had touched me, my dragon instantly decided she was mate material. Now I was in the throes of serious physical trauma. My heart galloped in my chest, heat bloomed across my skin, and the scent of her—vanilla, lavender, and the coffee she'd just sipped—lingered in my nose.

I should have foreseen this. We'd been flirting for weeks, and I'd grown attached to the curious blonde with the voluptuous curves and raging ambition. Her coming in here was the best part of my day. I'd been fooling myself to think I could keep her in the friend zone. Not with this pull between us. I was a hair trigger from throwing her over my shoulder and fucking her on the desk in the backroom.

"I should..." I trailed off, incapable of looking away from her or thinking of a single thing I had to do other than fuck her.

She looked around the empty café. "I think you can take a break if you aren't feeling well. It's started to rain." She pointed at the drops beating a rhythm against the window. "No wonder it's dead tonight. No one in Thornsboro leaves their house when it's cold and stormy. At least not at this time of year. The roads can get icy."

And she hated the rain. It was raining the night her mother died. I should've been comforting her. My dragon swelled within me, his voice ringing in my ear like that Marvel character who's possessed by an alien. *She'd feel safe under you,* he growled. He coiled and chuffed within me.

"Uh..." I pulled the beany from my head, tossed it on the back counter, and ran a hand through my wild hair.

"Hey, are you sure you're okay?"

"I'm okay. I'm just... running a little hot." God, wasn't that the truth? Sometimes I even breathed fire. I needed to change the subject. Distraction was the only thing that was going to work in this situation.

"Why don't you, uh, tell me about this story you've been working on?" I folded my arms across my chest, thankful that the high counters hid everything that was happening from the waist down.

She gave a proud, ear-to-ear smile. "It all started the first time I came in here. Someone had left a *Washington Post* on the table—I think it was Pembrooke—so I picked it up because I love to read the news in the papery flesh."

"I remember." I was barely able to follow what she was saying around the drum of my blood pounding in my veins.

"There was a picture of Supreme Court Justice Shiller on the cover, and in the very corner of the photo was a ring, like a class ring, on his finger. Somehow—like magic, really, when you consider the odds—I remembered seeing the same ring on the finger of Senator Cromwell during an interview he did with CNN. I did a reverse image search on a blown-up version of this ring and started looking for it in all the major news outlets. Not only was I able to make a list of over a dozen influential men with the same ring, but I was also able to find a photo clear enough for me to make out an inscription on the face of the ring. '*Astra inclinant, sed non obligant.*'"

Oh shit. "The stars incline us, they do not bind us," I translated, my skin chilling from the implications. The motto was an affront to dragons, who took their guidance from the stars. We weren't bound by them either, but the Saint's Order liked to pretend we were robots, lower-level thinkers who were slaves to meaningless celestial phenomenon.

Reagan gave a delighted laugh. "Exactly. How did you know? I had to use a translation app. I should have just asked you." She pushed a curl of her blond hair behind her shoulder. "Anyway, after a truly interesting trip down the rabbit hole of the internet, I started following dozens of ultrarich people related to those with these rings like a hound dog. Imani cracked the dark web and found a name. They're all part of a secret society known as the Saint's Order. It's like Yale's Skull and Bones, but I think maybe bigger. They're not tied to any specific university, just powerful people. Illuminati level."

The Saint's Order was nothing like Skull and Bones. They were killers. I swallowed hard. I should be thankful for the chills I was getting because they were doing a good job curbing my dragon's lustful energy.

She grinned. "Anyway, one of the business owners I followed has a wife who does his promotional videos, and she was complaining that he was traveling to Harpers Ferry for what she called a boys' night. I thought that was weird, so I started calling everyone on my list and asking for an appointment for the same date, and all of them are busy next Friday, Mason. I think they're all going to be in Harpers Ferry for a meeting of the society, and I plan to be there with video cameras. I'm going to expose the Saint's Order to the world."

I didn't know what to say, so I scratched the back of

my neck, trying to think of some way to stop her from pursuing this. "So, they're like the Freemasons." They were nothing like the Freemasons, but downplaying the importance of the Order would be the only way she might lose interest.

"I think this is something more," she said confidently. "My theory is that this Order is an association of the richest people in the world, willing to do anything to maintain their hold on the majority of the world's wealth. I'm think they are a secret oligarchy influencing everything in our country."

Try the world, I corrected in my head. She was so excited she was practically vibrating in her seat.

This was a disaster. In an ironic twist of fate, my presence had helped her connect the dots leading directly to a society of killers. The Saint's Order had been hunting my kind for hundreds of years, since Saint George famously slew the dragon and the most powerful humans collaborated to wage war against us. Dragons like me sparked innovation and freethinking in humans. It's why we were sent here by the creator. Our presence among humans spawned their creativity but also brought change and revolution. And when you were at the top, born into wealth and power, the last thing you wanted was a disruption in the order of things.

Every time Reagan had come into the cafe, my energy had helped her reach her goals, and that was a problem. Because I hadn't realized until now that her goal was exposing the Saint's Order. Doing so could also expose my kind, and that would be a disaster of epic proportions.

"Listen, Reagan, I don't think you should pursue this meeting in Harpers Ferry." I tried to keep my voice friendly and light.

"Are you kidding? Of course I'm going to go." She leaned across her cappuccino. "Here's what I'm thinking. There are only so many places in Harpers Ferry big enough to house a gathering of this size. I'm going to go early and try to spot one of the members in town." I hated that idea and wanted to say something, anything, to get her to change her plans, but she grasped my hand and my mind went completely blank. "I just want to thank you, Mason. I swear your coffee and your friendship made all the difference."

Her touch did things to my insides I'd never felt before. My inner dragon arched against the inside of my skin, urging me to mate with her. Gods, the beast was an asshole, all animal instinct and almost impossible to control during my alignment. I tugged at the collar of my shirt. Blood pounded in my ears. Her touch felt so good against my skin I almost couldn't believe it was real. I wanted it on me. I wanted it everywhere. I wanted to feel her fingers wrapped around my cock.

"Mason? Are you sure everything's all right?"

I couldn't take it anymore. Reaching out, I cupped the back of her neck, closed the space between us, and kissed her. Goddamn, her lips were soft. I buried my fingers in her blond waves and swallowed her moan. As soon as her lips parted, I licked into her mouth, thrust and stroked against her tongue, then repositioned to probe deeper. My dragon growled when she pulled away.

"Oh my god," she said, panting. "I wondered when you'd do that. I mean, we've been training for Olympic flirt trials for weeks. Technically we've never been on a date but we've dated, if you count talking over my coffee as dating. I mean, I've told you things, and you've told me things. There are commonalities. But you're kind of quiet. I mean, you don't really say much, right? I wasn't sure if you felt the same way." She was babbling. I'd noticed she did that when she was nervous. Endearing.

I pinched her wagging chin gently and cut her off with another deep kiss over the counter. And then my dragon was in the driver's seat. I swept her cup aside and lifted her, setting her down on my side of the counter, one leg on either side of the rock-hard erection I was sporting.

"How the hell did you do that? You lifted me like I was made of air." She took my face in her hands.

Grabbing her hips, I scooted her ass to the edge and ground myself against her. "I was highly motivated," I mumbled. *Fuck.* This was happening. My beast wanted her and wanted her now. I ran my hand up the inside of her sweater and cupped the lacy fullness of her bra-covered breast. Thumbing her hardening nipple, I went in for another kiss, rubbing myself hard against her center. I trailed kisses down the side of her neck.

"Jesus Christ, Mason. You go from not able to date to humping me on the counter? I think

I have whiplash."

"Do you want me to stop?" I murmured. She'd have to tell me. I'd never be able to rein in my dragon without her explicit command.

"No." She scoffed, her eyes growing hooded. "I want you to take me somewhere we can do this for real."

Oh, I would take her. I'd carry her in the back, pin her against the nearest wall, and—

I was saved from that very bad idea when the bell above the front door chimed and Mr. Pembrooke from across the street strode in, wiping his rain-slicked boots on the mat.

I helped Reagan off the counter and said, "There you go. As good as new."

Pembrooke raised an eyebrow.

"She stepped on glass," I said loudly for his benefit. She gave me a secretive grin and rounded the counter to her seat.

"So, uh, would you like to meet up after close tonight?" she whispered.

"Sure. Give me your number. I'll stop by." I handed her my phone to type in her digits while I served Pembrooke, then circled back around once he was settled in with his chamomile tea.

"I texted myself from your phone, so now I have yours too," she said through the sexiest grin I'd ever seen.

"So, your place?" I asked.

Her face fell. "Actually, I still live with my dad. Not for long though. I'm signing a lease on a new place next week, that apartment above Whitman's Hardware.

That's part of the reason I need this story. It's going to be tight until I can get promoted at the *Independent*."

I tucked her hair behind her ear while I tried to suppress the protective instinct that roared within me at the thought of her living alone above the hardware store. Our eyes met and held, and my body lit up like a string of Christmas lights. Yeah, I might be standing guard outside her door each night. Better yet, from beside her in bed.

She sighed through her nose. "So... your place?"

I nodded.

"I have to run home and feed Litz."

"I'll text you the address. See you after I lock up." I didn't want her to leave. I didn't want her to move out of my reach.

The sultry smile she gave me as she padded toward the door made my heart skip and my inner dragon purr. "This is shaping up to be a very good day, Mason."

"I agree," I growled, my voice tinged with dragon fire.

Everything came back into focus once she was out the door. Without her scent in my nose and her body within reach, my logical mind was able to gain control of my dragon instincts. I went about my work, but the appetency grew increasingly worse every moment I wasn't touching her, and it felt like I had a bad flu by the end of my shift. I locked up the minute Pembrooke finished his tea and called my uncle Connor.

As a Zodiac Warrior, Connor was a defender of our race, one of twelve, each representing a sign of the zodiac so that at least one warrior would be at his strongest anytime we needed protection. He knew everything there was to know about the Saint's Order, and if anyone knew what to do in this situation, it would be him. I told him everything, even that I thought my dragon wanted Reagan as his mate.

"Damn it, Mason," he said once I'd explained it all. "What a fucking mess."

When Connor wasn't training, he ran a restaurant in Hell's Kitchen where his Aries intensity served him well. I was glad we weren't in the same room. I was big and could hold my own, but only the most reckless dragon would go head-to-head with Connor. The guy was intimidating as hell.

"What do you think I should do?"

"There's only one thing you *can* do. Get the fuck out of Dodge for the next thirty days. If you don't put some distance between you and her, your mating sickness will have you handing Reagan your balls as well as all our secrets."

"Yeah. I almost slipped up today. The thing is, I have feelings for her."

"Does she feel the same about you?"

"Maybe."

"Mating with a human is a big risk under the best of circumstances. Mating with a journalist who's investigating the Saint's Order is reckless. May I remind you that the peace accord between us does not extend to Order meeting grounds? If she goes to that meeting Friday, you can't go after her and you can't help her if she gets into trouble. If you do, it could be viewed as an act of war, and if you're captured, there's nothing me or the brotherhood can do to help you. You'll find yourself cuffed and owned by some Richie Rich tyrant or else face the hunt like your dad."

Mention of my father made me wince. "I won't go near Harpers Ferry. Believe me."

Connor snorted into the phone. "But you will, Mason, if you mate her. You're in your month of alignment. Your dragon has chosen her as a potential mate. This isn't just sex you're flirting with. If you have sex with her and your dragon seals the deal, you will crawl across broken glass if she asks you to. And you'll have to be chained up and behind bars to stop yourself from protecting her if she needs it. A mated dragon is a fucking weapon, Mason. Remember that."

"I will." My jaw clenched at the thought of leaving her, but I knew my uncle was right. It was for the best, for both of us. "I'll leave for Smoke Hole Canyon first thing in the morning."

"Good. I hear Andromeda is already there. If you haven't done the deed with Reagan yet, maybe there's still a chance you can redirect your dragon."

The thought made me nauseated. Andy was beautiful but like a sister to me. Besides, right then my dragon was writing Reagan's name on his notebook and surrounding it with doodle hearts. Stupid fucking beast.

"Thanks, man. See you at Mom's for the spring equinox."

"Call me if you need help, Mason. Appetency is nothing to mess with."

We said our goodbyes, and I ended the call. Then I found Reagan's number and texted her. *Sorry. Have to cancel. Sick.*

Her answer came back a second later. I thought you felt hot. Feel better soon.

Heart breaking and body aching for her, I grabbed a black Sharpie and a piece of paper from the office. I created a sign in the neatest block letters I could manage and hung it face out on the glass door.

DUE TO REASONS BEYOND OUR CONTROL, FORGE'S CAFÉ WILL BE CLOSED UNTIL MARCH 20TH.

Chapter Nine

REAGAN

I couldn't sleep. Mason's text had thrown my mood off considerably. I wasn't sure what to make of it. On the one hand, he *had* felt feverish to me, and his face had paled a few times during our conversation. But damn it, he sure didn't seem sick when he lifted me onto the counter and humped me within an inch of an orgasm.

I couldn't help but wonder if his earlier reservations about us had come back full force once I'd left Forge's. Sighing, I turned over in bed, sawing my legs under the covers. There was only one way to find out if he was really sick or if I should take this personally, and that was to ask him face-to-face tomorrow.

A crack of lightning lit up my bedroom, followed by the rumble of distant thunder. Litz lurched in his dog pillow, then ran to me, jumping onto the bed and burying his face in my armpit. "It's okay, boy." I ran my hand soothingly along his spine.

My mother died during weather like this. The storm itself had nothing to do with her death. Her heart simply stopped beating. We learned from the autopsy that she'd had a heart defect as a child, one that was never properly diagnosed. It triggered a massive heart attack that killed her instantly.

That night the thunder and lightning had rattled the windows as I watched the paramedics carry her body, out to the waiting ambulance. The rain had soaked her white nightgown. Her body appeared frail underneath, as if death had long since moved in. That last rain-soaked image of my mother was burned into my young brain and the memory came back to me in vibrant technicolor now.

I hated storms.

Closing my eyes, I tried to force myself back to sleep, snuggling Litz against my side, but all I could see behind my closed lids was my mother's body on the gurney, her lack of reaction to the rain hitting her face. This was ridiculous. It happened over a decade ago. I needed to let it go. Gathering Litz into my arms, I took a fortifying breath and climbed out of bed. Step by shaky step, I padded toward the window, resolved to face my fear. Litz wiggled, and I set him down near my feet. He jogged back to his pillow and lay down.

Although I couldn't see much of the yard through the darkness and sheeting rain, when lightning struck, it was like God turned the lights on. For a moment it was as bright as day. I stared through the pelting rain at the backyard as flashes came and went.

Crack. My breath caught in my throat. Rushing to the rain-slammed glass, I pressed myself against the window, willing the lightning to strike again. I could have sworn I'd seen Mason on the edge of our property, walking toward the house. He'd been too far away for me to see his face, but I knew his walk. No one else moved like that, with an almost predatory grace.

Palms pressed against the glass, I concentrated on the place I'd spotted him, but when another lightning strike lit up the night, he was gone. Shit, I had to be seeing things. What would he be doing here this time of night? And in a storm? Especially considering he was sick. He didn't even know where I lived.

Still, I watched until I no longer trembled when the thunder rolled through me and I'd memorized every detail of the yard. With a smile on my face, I lay back in bed, realizing that Mason had somehow broken me of my fear tonight without even being here. Just the thought of him had been enough of a distraction to make me forget my worries. I licked my lips, remembering the way he'd kissed me—uninhibited, savage, potent. Everywhere his lips had pressed seemed to burn deep within my flesh. All I wanted was to do it again and more. For a minute there, I was convinced he planned to fuck me right on the counter.

Quietly, I laughed at myself. Something had to give. I'd lusted after Mason since the first day I'd met him in that café. And over the weeks I'd gotten to know him, I'd grown to care for him in a way I'd never cared for a man before. Maybe it was because he seemed different from most others in my life. I was so sick of people like my father with big egos and even bigger wallets. Mason had big-dick energy without having the big ego to go along with it. I didn't care if he was a wealthy man. Running a small-town café like Forge's was honest work, but likely not lucrative. What mattered was he was a *good* man. Thoughtful, creative, perceptive, and gorgeous as all hell.

Best of all, he wanted me and I wanted him. After that kiss, a relationship with Mason seemed inevitable, although what the boundaries of that relationship might be was still to be determined. I couldn't wait to stop by the café to see him again. First thing after work, I planned to pick up where I'd left off with my favorite barista.

Chapter Ten

MASON

Rain pelted the back of my head as I stood outside what I'd concluded was Reagan's bedroom window. I'd caught a glimpse of her as I entered the property. I didn't think she'd seen me given her weaker human eyes, the darkness, and the storm, but I'd camouflaged myself anyway before moving nearer.

Dragons are resistant to the weather. My skin barely felt the sting of the rain, and I had no trouble seeing through the sheeting water. If anything, the cold helped with the fever I'd been suffering from since the mating sickness kicked in. It also washed away any scent of Reagan from the yard, which was helping me do as Connor suggested and leave her alone. I *did* plan to depart for Smoke Hole Canyon first thing in the morning, but I needed to see her one more time.

The part of my soul that was my dragon whimpered

like a beaten dog within my chest. We wanted her like we'd never wanted anything. If I was honest with myself, I'd come here tonight in hopes of picking things up where we'd left off, at least in her mind.

Dragons enjoyed certain psychic abilities, one of them being dreamwalking. I could enter her mind while she slept and interact with her in her dreams. The promise of touching her one more time had been enough for me to look up where she lived and drive all the way out here. But now that I was standing outside her window, I was glad she was awake and that option was off the table. What I'd been considering was wrong and I knew it. Entering someone's mind without their permission was a violation. And even though my instincts told me she wouldn't mind a dream encounter with me, I shouldn't have even considered it.

My inner dragon howled in displeasure. He stormed inside my chest until I felt nauseated from his tirade. "Sorry, buddy, this one's not for you."

Reagan had her hands pressed against the glass, her breath fogging the space between them. Gods, she was beautiful. I'd always been a spiritual person, always trusted in where the universe was guiding me. Part of that was having a keen sense for right and wrong. I was doing the right thing leaving her—in my current state, I could hurt her delicate human flesh, and her pursuit of the Saints Order could definitely hurt me and my kind if we got too close. I was saving us both a ton of pain by leaving her tonight. But damn if it didn't hurt like someone was tearing my skin off.

Running a hand over my hair, I slicked off some of the water and started for my car, wishing I hadn't teased myself or my dragon with this excursion. Reagan had a brilliant life ahead of her. She had her story, her career, her friends, her new apartment. I'd done my part to inspire something great in her. I only wished I could stick around to see it.

Chapter Eleven

REAGAN

"The words don't magically appear on the screen, Reagan. You've got to actually press the keys." Imani leaned over my shoulder to get a better look at me, and I jolted out of the daydream I'd been having about Mason. As always, my gorgeous friend looked ready for a Paris runway with her long black braids and perfectly manicured nails. Today they were fuchsia and exactly matched her elegant, wide-legged jumpsuit.

I turned in my chair to give her my full attention. "Thanks. This obituary is never going to get written if I don't lock myself out of fantasyland." I took another swig of the dark swill I'd acquired from the break room, yearning for one of Mason's cappuccinos.

Imani's answering grin dripped with mischief, and she perched herself on the edge of my desk as if she was in no hurry to return to her own work. "What are you fantasizing about? Or should I ask *who* are you fanta-sizing about?"

I scraped my teeth along my bottom lip. "I kissed Mason last night."

"The five-alarm smoke show from Forge's?" The deer-in-headlights impersonation she put on wasn't exactly surprising considering last we'd discussed the man he'd just turned me down for a date. "I thought you asked him out and he said no?"

"I did ask him out. He turned me down flat. Said he wasn't in a place to date."

"Right. We speculated hiding out from a crime lord he'd wronged in the past."

"Or that he had a micropenis and didn't think I could handle it."

"Could you handle it?"

"It wouldn't be ideal, but the man has a tongue." I shrugged and Imani laughed. "Seriously, I genuinely like this man, and not just for what's in his pants, which based on what was pressed against me last night is jumbo-sized."

"Wooo! Really?"

I smirked. "There's more to him than that though. He's like thoughtful and unexpectedly deep. The kind of person who really sees you, you know? Not to mention, he inspires me."

Imani waggled her eyebrows. "Let's get back to his tongue and jumbo dick. You said he kissed you last night?"

"Like the password to his Bitcoin fortune was lodged in my throat."

"Jesus. How was it?"

"Fire. Pure, unadulterated hotness. If I could orgasm from uvula stimulation alone, it would have happened."

"Wow. Okay." She gave a low, throaty laugh. "So, what now? Did he agree to a date?"

I allowed my head to roll back on my neck like I couldn't support its weight anymore and moaned. "Noooo. A customer came in and interrupted us. We exchanged numbers and were supposed to meet up later, but he texted me that he was sick."

"Sick?" She seemed as skeptical as I was.

"He had felt a bit feverish when things were going down. I don't know. It was all very...weird."

Her palms clapped down on her thighs. "Hmmm. Keep me posted. I'd like a full report on this very news-worthy matter."

I laughed. "Hey, before you go. What are you doing next Friday?"

She lowered her chin. "I was planning to visit a club and find someone with whom to take my own tongue measure-ments. Why do I think you have other plans for me?"

"Because I need your skills. My investigation into the Saint's Order panned out. A gathering is happening in Harpers Ferry. They're all meeting there, Imani. We need to go with a camera and break this thing open."

"Seriously? All the names we talked about?"

"The biggest and the most influential in the country.

Patterson gave us the green light. I need video, but we'll have to be discreet."

"Shiiit. This is big." Imani tapped her chin. "I'll have to wire you with a hidden camera and bring my pocket-sized for video."

"You have that stuff?" The *Independent* definitely did not have hidden cameras in their arsenal or their budget.

"Hell yeah. I'm a Black woman in America, honey. You never know when there's something you'll need to secretly record."

"Then let's blow this story and become so famous even our dogs have their own inground pools." I gave her a fist bump.

She snorted. "Your dog already does have his own pool. You forget I've spent a day on a floaty at Casa de Bailey."

The heaviness of impending change wrapped around me, and my smile faltered. "Not for long. I've decided to lease that place above Whitman's Hardware. It's the size of my current closet, but I can afford it and Mr. Whitman said he'd make an exception for Litz."

Her lips pressed together. "Couldn't work it out with your dad, huh?"

I shook my head. "I didn't try. This is my decision. He's a powerful man who's used to getting what he wants, and he's been trying to rope me into working for Bailey Enterprises since high school. If I hadn't had a scholarship, I don't know that he'd have paid for my journalism degree, you know? And it's become this bone of contention between us. Moving out is the only way I'll ever get him to view me as an adult and the only way we'll ever have a real relationship. Once he knows, beyond a shadow of a doubt, that I won't be working for Bailey, we can finally move beyond it and start being a family again."

She pulled me into a tight hug. "You're doing the right thing, girl, but let's get this story done so you're not living in the Whitman attic any longer than necessary." She pointed at my screen. "Now back to work. Girls who don't meet their deadlines don't get to follow up on hot barista kisses."

I turned back to my computer, typing like the keyboard was on fire.

By 4:59, I'd already wrapped up my work and checked in with Patterson. A quick stop in the restroom to fluff my hair and brush my teeth and I was on my way to Forge's, practicing what I'd say to Mason in my head if it turned out the sickness was an excuse.

"I know you said you can't get involved with anyone right now, but after last night, aren't we already involved?" I said to my steering wheel. I cleared my throat and tried another tack. "What if we did one of those no-strings-attached things? Friends with bene-fits?" Not ideal, but I'd try it if he would. I cracked my neck. "Maybe you can't get involved, but after last night, I think you owe me a beer." Yeah, that was the one. If I could get him alone, loosen his tongue with some alco-hol, I could find out his secret. Why had he really moved here? Why couldn't he get involved with anyone?

But when I reached Forge's, I noticed right away that

something was wrong. All the lights were off in the building, and there was no one in the parking lot. I parked and walked up to the door, testing it and finding it locked. Only then did I notice the handwritten sign on the door.

"Says he's gone for a month!" Mr. Pembrooke called from his porch across the street.

I marched over to him. "Did he tell you why?"

He shook his head. "Found out from the sign, same as you. Strange if you ask me."

"Yeah." I tucked my hair behind my ear. "He said he felt sick last night. Do you think that has something to do with it?"

Pembrooke shrugged. "What kind of sickness lasts exactly a month?"

"Good point." I turned to walk back to my car.

"You could check on him. He's renting the old Wilson cottage."

"That's right." I remembered him mentioning that once. "Hey, how do you know where he lives?"

He laughed. "It's a small town, girly. Talk to someone every now and then."

"Nice chatting with you Mr. Pembrooke."

He raised one hand and gave me a wave.

Chapter Twelve

REAGAN

I texted Mason that I'd seen the sign and asked directly if he was okay. The text was delivered but not read. I texted him again, mentioning I was worried about him. Then I texted him again and said I was worried about me. After all, we'd played tonsil hockey. If he had something contagious, I should know. We were living in the age of Covid after all. When Sunday came around, I'd had enough. I drove out to the old Wilson place.

"You do realize this is bordering on stalking, right?" Imani asked.

I'd called her to test out all the reasons I thought a personal drop-in visit to Mason was appropriate. She wasn't buying it.

"Just a friend checking on a friend," I said.

"A friend checking on a friend with an unlisted number and address."

"Hey, we exchanged numbers and as for the address part, he told me once where he lived. Mr. Pembrook simply confirmed it."

"If he'd wanted you to stop by, he would have invited you," she singsonged.

"I'm investigating. His behavior is suspicious," I countered. "I'm trying to find out why he hasn't contacted me concerning my probable infection if what he said was true and he's sick.

And if he lied, I deserve an explanation."

"Why didn't you just call?"

"I did. And texted. A lot."

"Oh dear."

"And left messages."

"Oh, Reagan. This guy ghosted you, honey. Back away slowly."

"Yeah, well, I'm here. Wish me luck."

"Luck, I guess. Is it too late for me to talk you out of this?"

"Bye," I mumbled and hung up. Once I'd stuffed my phone into my bag, I rapped on the door and waited. No answer. I knocked again. Waited. Nothing. Not a sound from inside. A chill climbed my spine. What if the reason Mason hadn't reached out was because he couldn't? What if he was too sick, or even... God forbid... dead?

I shuffled around the side of the quaint little log-cabin-style cottage and cupped my hands around my eyes to peek into his side window. What I saw didn't put me at ease. No signs of life. Bristling, I pressed my palms against the glass and pushed up. The window cracked open an inch.

"Jackpot."

I dug my fingers under the edge and lifted, opening the window wider, then hoisted myself through the opening, wriggling headfirst into what looked like the living room. I landed with a grunt on the cushions of a sage-colored, overstuffed sofa.

"Mason?" I called, climbing to my feet and navigating to the bedrooms. He wasn't in either of them, but multiple drawers were hanging open like he'd packed in a hurry. I checked the closet and then the bathroom. I ended up back in the living room, turning circles. The place wasn't that big.

Mason Forge was not in this cottage.

On a hunch, I went to the kitchen and opened the fridge. Empty. The garbage? Empty. So he'd left. But why? Where had he gone?

I strode back toward the living room, noticing something leaning against the oversized sofa. I hadn't seen it there before, under the shadow of the arm. Couldn't have seen it if I hadn't walked into the kitchen. Carefully, I pulled it out to get a better look.

"A sleeping bag? What the fuck?" I turned the thing over. Why would Mason have a sleeping bag leaning against his sofa? I sat down on the coffee table and went over what I knew for sure. Mason left a note he'd be gone a month. He left in a rush, but the way his fridge was cleaned out, it was premeditated. He didn't mean to come back anytime soon. He'd left a sleeping bag out like he'd meant to pack it but forgot. A sleeping bag wasn't something you left out in your living room. It was a closet item, right?

Why hadn't he mentioned where he was going? Where the fuck did he go? Was he even sick?

"No, you idiot," I whispered to myself. It didn't take a giant mental leap to assume he'd told me he was sick to let me down easy. If he had been sick, I suppose he could have gone to a relative's house to recover, but who cleaned out their fridge for that? No, this was something else. He was running, but from what? "Where did you go, Mason? And why?"

The cottage even smelled like Mason—smoke and spice with a hint of coffee grounds. I leaned my head back on the plush, overstuffed sofa and breathed in deep. The couch was the kind of furniture that partially swallowed you when you sat on it and had a decidedly man-cave aesthetic. There wasn't one chair or sofa this comfortable in my entire professionally decorated house. I sagged into it while I waited for my brain to produce ideas about how to find Mason.

I tried to think back if he'd given me any clues to where he might go. His place was sparsely decorated. Actually, now that I looked around, I guessed most of this came with the cottage. It looked dated, and he'd only lived in Thornsboro a short time. One thing stood out to me though, something I knew wasn't here before. There was a large, framed photograph on the wall—an aerial shot of Smoke Hole Canyon, labeled as such in the lower right-hand corner. The detail was stunning. Either the photographer had one hell of a lens or it was taken by a low flying plane. More importantly, it was the only picture in the living room. Otherwise, the walls were conspicuously bare.

My eyes fell on the sleeping bag again. I stood to give the room another once-over. When I climbed out of the poufy couch-hole, I noticed the glint of bright blue foil under the sofa. Capturing the corner of it with my toe, I slid it out into the open. A packet. I lifted it, inspecting both sides. Dehydrated stew, the kind used on camping trips.

I furrowed my brow. The living area wasn't messy. The carpet was vacuumed and there wasn't any clutter, but the two things left out were camping supplies. This was the room of a man who'd packed hastily for an outdoor trip, during the wettest, iciest February we'd had in years.

What the actual fuck? He'd told me he was sick to go... camping? My eyes locked on the photograph. What happened next was weird. Inexplicable. Deep inside my chest, behind my sternum, I felt a tug. I wanted to be there, in Smoke Hole Canyon, and my every instinct, my every living cell, screamed at me that Mason was there too. It was a crazy, Hail Mary pass of an idea. I stood and swept the sleeping bag into my arms.

Going after him was a mistake. He might not even be there. The entire idea was certifiable and more than a little stalkerish. If I did come across Mason, he might immediately write me off as a crazy predator and reject me outright. I understood what I was doing was socially awkward and unreasonable. If I was a friend, I'd tell that friend to stay put and let this go.

And I didn't care one bit. My curiosity was off the charts. Good or bad, I had to know the truth. And my gut told me I'd find it in Smoke Hole Canyon.

Chapter Thirteen

MASON

Whatever was in the red Solo cup in my hand must have been strong because even my dragon was feeling tipsy. I had the distinct feeling that if I had to sprout wings and fly right now, I'd probably bounce off the side of the cavern a few times before I caught air. The cave we were in had taken on a soft, hazy quality, and I didn't think it was from the smoke coming off the central fire.

"Hey, what's in this?" I asked Andy. I'd known the cute, dark-haired dragon since we were children. She'd been glued to my side since we'd arrived, trying to avoid Alex, another Pisces dragon who had a hard time taking no for an answer. It was good to have a friend here. I was still pretty shaken by the past twenty-four hours.

"Jay calls it dragon-fire tea." She blew over the top of her cup, and her breath ignited the fumes, sending a plume of fire toward the ceiling of the cave. "I saw him dump a jug of fireball in there along with some vodka, tequila, and gin."

I gazed into the murky depths of my glass and chuckled. "Anything nonalcoholic in the mix? Did he even cut it with ice?"

She shrugged. "I think I taste lemonade... or maybe orange? It's hard to tell if that part is zero proof or not. Could be the flavor of the vodka."

"Hmm. I'm having flashbacks to my college days. I hope I'm not headed for the same unfortunate end. I'd rather not taste this on the way back up. Plus, I don't have the benefit of a porcelain throne to rest my head against." It took a lot to get a dragon of my size drunk, but I'd been pounding these things since I arrived. I decided to slow down. I planned to fly back to my own cave to sleep, and I needed to be sober enough to find it. I set my cup down and turned my attention back to the fire. The soothing crackle of the burning logs was drowned out by a dozen or so Pisces dragons chatting as they milled around it.

Looking into her own cup, Andy's smile faded. "At least it takes the edge off the appetency."

I glanced in her direction. She was right about that. On a scale of normal to ready to hump a stalactite, I was at about a five out of ten. I wasn't in danger of losing control on an inanimate object, but the thought wasn't particularly unappealing.

"Looks like Alex would be happy to take the edge off for you." I smirked, darting a glance at the blond dragon across the cave who hadn't taken his eyes off Andy since she'd arrived.

"Ugh. No, thank you." She stuck her tongue out.

I laughed. "He's in good shape. Shit, he looks even more stacked than last year."

"That's because he has Napoleon syndrome."

"Hmm?"

"You know, he's compensating for his inferior... size."

I winced. "Ouch. Short people have feelings too."

"I wasn't talking about his height."

We both chortled like we were still in eighth grade. "Please tell me you don't know that from personal experience."

Her smile faded. "I felt it when he pressed me up against the wall last year. I had to pop him in the jaw to keep him from riding my leg like a dog."

"He's still interested after that?"

She snorted. "I think he liked it."

Alex's unflinching gaze started weirding me out and I turned, blocking his view of Andy. "So, uh, mating sickness. Is yours worse this year?"

"It gets worse every year." Her face grew somber. "I'm going to be twenty-nine and if I don't find a mate soon, I'm seriously considering asking the doc to put me in a chemically induced coma for the month."

"Have you gone to see the Oracle?"

"No. Why, so she can stare up at the stars and give me some vague generalization about the dragon I'm waiting for?" Raising one finger, she made her voice hollow and mysterious. "You will fall in love sometime between the mating of the wild pheasant and the arrival of the phoenix comet fifteen years from now. He will appear to you in the presence of a flower."

I laughed until my sides hurt. "Yeah. She's the reason I'm living in Thornsboro. Although... I guess her guidance was spot on in a way."

"Hmm? How so?"

Was I really doing this? Was I really going to admit what happened with Reagan? I needed to talk about it, and if there was one person I could trust, it was Andy. "I felt the call."

Andy's mouth dropped open. "You felt the call of your one true mate? What the fuck are you doing here? Why aren't you with her?"

"I didn't claim her."

Tucking a strand of hair behind her ear, she scoffed incredulously. "You experienced the invitation to mate, during your alignment no less, and you didn't claim her? Why? You could be free of this... pain." She spread a hand over her chest, and I knew exactly the pain she was talking about. I ached, soul deep. My desire for sex was a gnawing hunger. It hurt. A lot. Every hour I didn't get off, the worse it grew.

I shifted my lower jaw, trying to loosen a muscle that I was afraid might snap. "She's human."

Casting a pitying look in my direction, Andy folded her arms. "So what? I mean, it's inconvenient. Not ideal for sure. You'd have to be careful with her and you'd need permission from the Oracle to make it official. But it's not as if you'd be the first dragon to mate a human."

I sighed, my eyes giving a lazy roll at how simple she made it sound. "She's also a journalist, and her life's work is to break a major news story."

"Ugh. That does complicate things. Is she loyal? Do you think she'd keep your secret?"

"There's more," I said. "She's been investigating the Saint's Order and is on the verge of uncovering exactly what they're all about. In fact, she's planning to attend a gathering undercover this Friday."

Andy lowered herself to sit on the edge of a rock. "Whoa."

"Yeah. If I mate her, there's no way my dragon will let her go in there alone, and if I cross the boundary—"

"You're as good as theirs. *If* they don't believe it's an act of war and kill you outright, considering you have warrior blood." She scowled.

"On the nose."

"So that's why you're here... to try to make it through your alignment without claiming her because if you claim her, not only will she know what you are, but she'll definitely put together our kind's relationship with the Saint's Order. And if she chooses to still go to the gathering, you'll be in mortal danger. Plus, she'd be in a prime position to take our secret public, and you can't let that happen."

"Even without claiming her, I might not be capable of letting her walk in there alone. Not after what happened to my father."

"That's majorly shitty."

"Yeah. If we did mate, you know I'd be expected to

completely wipe her mind if she pursued the story anyway. Then I'd be mated to a person with a hole in the middle of them. If I could even preserve the relationship, I'd be forced to watch as she dragged herself through her days, wondering why she felt like a piece of her was missing. This project is not a small thing to her. It's her dream and represents her independence from her father."

"Gods. So, in summary, your plan is to keep your distance and let things happen as if you weren't in her life... by staying out of her life. I'm so sorry, Mason. You must have real feelings for her, beyond the mating instinct, to suffer like this for her happiness. You love her too much to doom her to a life under your dragon's protection."

I picked up my cup, but it was empty. The conversation had reopened a raw wound, and the effects of the alcohol were already wearing off. "Unfortunately, I believe your assessment is correct, although I think the use of the *L* word is premature." She took a deep breath, her expression filling with sympathy.

"I have a proposal," she said, staring into her own empty cup.

"Yeah?"

Her expression grew serious, her eyes darkening. "Why don't we use each other?"

I shook my head at the ridiculous notion. "You're my oldest friend. It would be like being with my sister."

"But I'm not your sister. And I'm safe. I'm not your

mate, and you're not mine. We both know each other's boundaries. There wouldn't be complications."

I tried to picture it. Andy was beautiful, and for a moment I allowed my thoughts to drift to what it would be like to have her under me. From a purely intellectual standpoint, it wasn't a bad idea. But despite my appetency, I had absolutely nothing going on downstairs at the thought. I hadn't thought anything could eliminate the perpetual hard-on I'd had after kissing Reagan, but the thought of being with Andy did. It was like a bucket of ice water.

"I'm sorry. No. I can't."

A soft smile turned her lips. "You're already hers."

I leaned the side of my head against the cave wall. "Maybe."

We stood there, absorbing each other's silence, until the distant sound of a woman's scream met my ears. A scream my dragon was sure was Reagan Bailey's.

Chapter Fourteen

REAGAN

This was the dumbest idea I'd ever had. I leaned against the trunk of my Jetta in a random campsite parking lot and stared up at the stars. Smoke Hole Canyon and the surrounding campgrounds covered a sprawling distance. Even if I were one hundred percent sure that Mason was here, the chances of me finding him, especially at night, were close to nil. And that's not even considering that he might not want to see me. I'd sent him a dozen texts over the last several days, and he hadn't returned any of them.

Which begged the question: why the hell was I here, in the dead of winter, with a man's sleeping bag in my trunk? I was not this woman! I pressed my mittened hands over my face as tears breached my eyelids. I hated this thing inside me. It was as if he'd tied a bungee cord to my heart when he'd kissed me, and since then, all I could think of was how to get back to him and alleviate this incessant tug connecting us. It was driving me crazy.

Frustrated beyond reason, I looked up at the stars and screamed.

It wasn't like anyone could hear me. Absolutely no one was camping here this time of year. It was freezing. Now that I'd reached the parking lot, everything I'd felt in Mason's cottage seemed ludicrous. I was turning into a madwoman over a goddamned crush!

With a deep sigh, I started to get back into my car... and almost jumped out of my skin. Mason was standing in the tree line like he'd manifested from the shadows, his eyes glinting yellow as a cat's in the moonlight.

"What are you doing here?" he asked, his voice harsh and raspy like he needed a drink. Damn it. He was angry. My huge mistake was growing ever more complicated.

"I... I, uh... I brought you your sleeping bag?" It came out like a question even though I'd meant it as a statement. I opened my trunk and threw the roll at him. He caught it and tucked it under one arm, his eyes narrowing.

"How is it you have my sleeping bag?" The words came out like a growl, and I had the unhinged temptation to simply jump in my car and drive away as quickly as possible. But I'd driven all the way out here. If I ran now, what would be the point of all this?

"I broke into your cottage," I admitted.

No reaction. Mason stared at me impassively. Was he even blinking?

"I saw the sign on Forge's. Mr. Pembrooke told me

you were renting the old Wilson place. You'd mentioned it to me once, so I knew he was right. When you didn't return my texts, I worried you were dead because you'd said you were sick. You looked sick, Mason. Really sick. Why aren't you sick? So, I pushed open your window—which wasn't locked by the way, even though it really should have been. Just because we live in a small town doesn't mean you can trust your neighbors. And...and, I had to let myself inside to make sure you were okay, only you weren't there. And I saw the sleeping bag and came to bring it to you." I was rambling again. Jesus. Every time I was nervous, words poured out of me like verbal diarrhea.

For a second we just stared at each other. I reached for the door handle again.

"How did you know I'd be *here*?"

"The picture on your wall." The more I thought about that, the weaker that evidence seemed, and when he narrowed his eyes, scrutinizing me, I realized how far-fetched that sounded. "I guess I didn't know *exactly*. I had a hunch, okay? A weird... A really bizarre feeling." My brow furrowed as I rubbed the spot over my sternum that had felt tight during the incident. Fuck. Now I really sounded like a stalker. I turned the conversation around. "You should have told me you were leaving. I had no idea what kind of sick you were or if you were contagious. We kissed. You might have infected me. It was rude."

"I'm not... I don't have anything contagious," he gritted out.

"Oh." Just as I suspected. "Was this just...? Did you just want to go camping... for a month... in February?"

One sharp nod. That's all the explanation he gave.

"Are you on the run from the mob?" I blurted.

He snorted, then gave a deep laugh. "No."

That's it. Just no. This guy was killing me. "Do you have a micropenis or some other physical deformity you're hiding from me?"

His expression darkened. "We were close enough on that counter for you to know."

"Then what is going on?" I asked half-heartedly. I'd given up any hope of getting a straight answer. Rejection, humiliation, and anger left me feeling sick. I took a deep breath and blew it out slowly, then reached for the door handle yet again. "All right. You have your sleeping bag now, so I'll... uh..."

His hand gripped my wrist. How the hell had he gotten to me so fast? One moment he was at the tree line, the next he'd dropped the sleeping bag and had his fingers wrapped around me. I lifted my gaze from his grip to those blue eyes that threatened to drown me in their depths.

"How did you know where to find me?" he asked again.

"I... I told you. It was... intuition." I rubbed my chest again, thinking about the ache. It was gone now. "This is where I expected you to be."

The cold air stung my cheeks, but when his hand landed over my heart, it felt warm and heavy, even through my puffer. How was he so hot when he wasn't even wearing a coat?

"You felt it here?" His breath brushed my lips, sending my heart fluttering.

I bit my lip. "Crazy, huh?" Now he'd definitely believe I was a stalker.

He stepped in closer, backing me against the side of the car. This close, I realized he was a good foot taller than me, and I had to crane my neck to maintain eye contact.

"You should leave," he said, his voice distracted and unconvincing. Even if I'd wanted to go, I'd have to push him out of the way to open the door, and that was the last thing I wanted to do. I wanted to stay right here, pressed against this giant of a man who even out here smelled of smoke and spice. Cinnamon sticks on an open fire. I breathed deeply of him.

"Yeah, I should go," I said weakly. I stepped one foot out, spreading my legs farther apart and used my mittened hands to grip his hips, settling his weight flush against me. I tilted my pelvis at the same time I pulled him closer, gaining some degree of comfort from the enormous erection that pressed into my abdomen. His body certainly didn't want me to go. "If you want me to leave, you'll have to move out of the way."

A low growl rumbled in his chest, as it had the first night he'd kissed me, and I tilted my head back to look up at him through hooded eyes. What I saw in his face was absolutely predatory. Something deep inside me, some Paleolithic instinct in my DNA, urged me to run, while another part, a bigger part, loved the thrill of being the target of his intense focus. My nipples hardened, and my core grew warm and achy with need. I sighed softly and lifted on my toes to bring my lips closer to his.

The growling grew louder. "Reagan, if you don't leave now, I won't be able to control myself." A bead of sweat formed on his temple despite the cold. Jesus, how badly did he want me? "There are things about me... dark things you don't want to see. I'll take you, and I won't be gentle about it." He swallowed hard enough that I could hear it. "Do you know how much I want you?"

"Tell me," I said breathlessly.

"Enough to peel those leggings off your body, bend you over, and bury myself inside you right here in the parking lot. Do you understand?"

My lips hovered dangerously close to his. "Dark things, huh? I seem to be having some dark thoughts myself." I'd grown instantly wet the moment he touched me, but the blunt manner he addressed me lit a fire in my veins. My pussy throbbed, needing to be touched. God, he was gorgeous, and it felt like I'd wanted him forever. The thought of him taking me from behind made me melt like butter.

He closed his eyes, a tremor going through him. "Reagan..."

I licked my lips. "I don't want to leave," I said breathlessly, brushing my lips against his. "I want you, Mason. I've wanted you for a long time. If you want to take me, take me!"

I thought he was going to kiss me. Instead, he pushed

off the car and backed away. His nostrils flared and his fingers trembled. *For me.* He wanted me so badly he was shaking. I was trembling too.

"Last chance. Get in your car and go." He raised both hands. "Move very slowly."

I chewed my lip. That was the last thing I wanted to do. Straightening up, I placed a hand on the door handle, considering what he'd told me to do. I spotted a hiking path that branched off the parking area. He must have come from that direction. Did he have a tent back there? A bed? I gave him a long, hot look over my shoulder. I was not chickening out. Not after that kiss. Not after coming all this way. Not when he was looking at me like I was a healing elixir and he was a dying man.

"I have a better idea," I said, sending him a dark glance. "If you catch me, you can have me."

I launched myself onto the trail at a full run.

The sound that came from Mason's chest was feral. I'd never heard a man make that noise. And then his feet were falling hard and fast behind mine. I pushed myself into a sprint, heart galloping and breath coming in pants, but he gained on me quickly. A laugh bubbled up my throat as I weaved and raced ahead, thankful for the moon to light my way. He was so close behind me now, I could practically feel the heat coming off his body. Only his breathing wasn't labored as mine was, and by the sound of his footsteps on my heels, he could catch me anytime he wanted to.

A frisson of fear traveled through me, the kind of fear you get when you're at the top of a roller coaster, staring over the edge. Exhilaration had me tearing my mittens off my sweating hands and shoving them in my pockets as I ran. The movement slowed my stride, and his foot landed next to mine. Shit, he'd almost run right over me.

I laughed harder. My thighs were starting to burn, and I glanced over my shoulder at him. He wasn't laughing, but there was a wicked smirk on his face like he was toying with me, a cat with a mouse. He was going to catch me, and when he did... The thought made things deep within me clench. I wanted that. I wanted that so badly.

Oof. My toe caught on something, a stone or a root, and I went flying. My hands shot out to break my fall. I never hit the ground. A tree-branch-sized arm caught me around the waist before my palms met the dirt path.

"Thanks—" I started to say, but I was distracted by his frantic tugging at the waistband of my pants.

Holy fuck, I barely had my feet under me before he had my leggings stripped down to my ankles. His fingers plunged between my legs from behind. I was so wet it was embarrassing... almost. Clearly he was just as worked up. I moaned at his touch. I might have stopped running, but my heart hadn't slowed a bit. In fact, it was pounding so hard I thought it might explode. I couldn't catch my breath.

"Mmmm, mate," he crooned in my ear. His nose traced along the side of my neck, sending goose bumps marching across my skin. "You're ready for me."

Mate. I wasn't worried about the odd word choice. Every part of me was focused on the spot where his adept fingers now circled my clit. I spread my legs as far as I could, but my leggings were caught on my boots. I tried to stand up straight to toe them off, but his hand fisted the back of my head and bent me in half again. I steadied myself by gripping the trunk of a nearby tree, although I had no chance of falling, not with Mason's arm like a steel band around my waist.

"Did you forget what I promised I'd do to you?"

"No," I said breathlessly.

His hand worked between my legs again. So good. I ground myself against his touch.

"Changed your mind?" Two fingers dipped inside me and I bucked against his hand, using the tree as leverage.

"No," I gasped. "I want you, Mason."

The hand between my legs disappeared, leaving me cold. I heard a zipper and then the rustle of fabric. The blunt head of his cock replaced his fingers between my legs. A tremor traveled through me, every nerve coming alive at the feel of him at my entrance. This was really happening.

I glanced over my shoulder, the stars shining brightly behind his head, the cold stinging my exposed skin, and for the first time in my life felt a pure moment of *rightness*. I wanted this man, yes, but this was more. The tug that had persisted since our kiss eased into a warm liquid contentment.

Eyes locked with his, I spread my knees as far as I could and eased back onto his cock. I was soaking wet and ready, but enormous as he was, it took a full minute of working myself back and forth onto him before he was fully seated, and I was stretched to my limit. He filled me to that sweet edge between pleasure and pain. I gasped as I waited for my body to adjust.

Connected at last, I heard him release a breath laden with fulfilled longing, his eyes closing for several seconds as if being in me was exquisite torture. It turned me on to be wanted like that, and my inner muscles loosened in response. Slowly he eased out before entering me again with a sharp thrust that made me grunt. Again, he pulled out, then slammed into me again and again at a teasing, tantalizing pace.

His hand plunged into my hair, rolling my head on my neck. The slight pull ratcheted up the pleasure. I needed more. I thrust backward, my ass slapping his hips, and it was like I'd waved a red flag in front of a bull. He went from savoring me to swallowing me whole in a heartbeat. The arm around my waist tightened, and he unleashed himself, thrusting hard and fast into me.

"You're mine, Reagan. You're fucking mine!" he growled into my ear.

God, his voice didn't even sound human. I arched my back, changing the angle until each of his pounding thrusts hit me in just the right place. He reached around me, unzipped my coat, and yanked the collar to the side. And then he bit me, right where my neck met my shoulder. I cried out as the slight sting fed an orgasm that tore through me, blinding me with an explosion of light. My inner walls clenched against the massive invasion hammering me, driving higher, to a place I'd never been before with any man. He teased it out, pressing my clit with his fingers as he pistoned into me.

And still he didn't quit. I'd barely come down from the first orgasm when another barreled into me like a runaway train.

This time Mason followed me over. He cried out, hot jets of his seed filling me as he spasmed against my back. His erection kicked, and my inner walls milked him, wanting everything he had to give. My legs gave out, but he held me up, held me to him, even as his own legs started to tremble.

When he finally slid out of me, I felt cold for the first time. It couldn't be more than forty-five degrees out here.

"Stay there," he ordered. He yanked his sweater and T-shirt over his head, then used the T-shirt to clean me up.

"Thanks." It was only then that I even thought about the fact we hadn't used a condom. I figured that was why he was looking at me with wild, panicked eyes. "Don't worry. I'm on birth control."

He snorted. "I'm not worried."

I pulled up my pants. "Where's your campsite anyway? It's freezing."

A wild gleam sparked in his eyes, and he gave me a wicked smile. "I'll show you."

I squealed as he tossed me onto his back like a ruck-sack and took off down the trail.

Chapter Fifteen

MASON

During alignment, a dragon's inner beast is closer to the surface than any other time of year. Dragons like me can shift into our animal form anytime we please, but normally our two-legged selves are calling the shots. Not so when the sun is in our sign. Dragons are hardwired to breed, and the older a dragon gets, the stronger the desire. Genetically, alignment is the only time of year when we can procreate successfully, which causes an instinctive and savage need to copulate for four weeks out of the year.

Reproduction isn't as much of a priority to dragonkind as it was in the past. Our population is strong thanks to the peace accord with the Saint's Order. But the drive I was suffering from was innate. Even homosexual dragons experience appetency during their alignment.

When dragons are mated, their mates understand and service each other's needs. Sex a few times a day, and the inner dragon eases into the back seat again. But without a mate, without sex with someone of the dragon's choosing, our bodies war with themselves, the inner beast constantly vying for control. It ages us too. Dragons who never find a mate eventually go up in flames like a phoenix. I wasn't there yet, but every year the fever grew worse.

That's why, once a dragon finds a mate, they're *all* in and will do anything for the one who eases their pain. A mated dragon is a tightly wound, six-ton weapon that will protect and possess their mate until death or direct rejection.

Mating with Reagan had been a bad idea on many levels, the biggest being she didn't know what I was or what she was in for. I'd broken an unwritten rule of my kind by taking a human the way I did without first revealing what I was to her, without giving her a fully informed choice. It was wrong. But when she'd mentioned that the bond had brought her to me, I realized our connection was further along than I'd thought. Oh sure, she called it intuition, but really it was my dragon calling to her along the spiderweb of a bond I'd laid when I kissed her. And when she'd disobeyed me when I'd ordered her to leave and run away from me instead, it triggered my dragon's predatory instincts.

In that moment, I was in the back seat and the dragon was driving. It hadn't helped that I'd been drinking and the dragon-fire tea had already muffled my inhibitions. I hunted her down, the scent of her burning in my nose. She smelled of vanilla, lavender, and coffee.

I wanted her to smell of me.

Gods, when I'd buried myself inside her, it had been like coming home. The relief was overwhelming, like diving into cool water on the hottest day of the year. Then the pleasure had started, and I knew I was hers. Reagan was my new addiction, and I planned to indulge myself in her, consequences be damned. Whether she fully understood what she was getting into or not, she'd consented, and that was enough for my dragon. We'd mated her, and now she was ours.

"What are you doing?" she asked nervously from my back.

"You said you wanted to go to my campsite."

"Yes, but I didn't realize that included free climbing up the side of the canyon!" She eyed the mountain in front of me skeptically.

"Hang on tight. I won't let you fall." I grinned at her over my shoulder and launched myself onto the rock. It would have been faster to fly, but she wasn't ready to see my wings and I wasn't ready to show them to her, not while she was somewhere she could run from me.

Her legs squeezed tighter around my waist. "I wasn't planning on letting go." She looked down, squealed, and squeezed me tighter.

I chuckled. Climbing rocks as a dragon is as natural as breathing. We don't need a good hold. Our fingers jab into the rock and make our own. I held her arms to my chest with one hand and climbed with my other.

She buried her eyes in the crook of my neck. "Hey, what about your sleeping bag?"

"I'll get it later."

"Don't we, uh, need it?"

"I love that you're thinking about lying down with me."

She laughed. "Maybe I'm just worried about staying warm."

"We won't need it to sleep on. And as for the cold, I suspect you're warm enough right now, pressed against me."

I climbed faster. Reagan and I needed to have a conversation, and the faster we could have it, the faster I could be inside her again.

Her breath fanned across my skin. "You are incredibly warm. Are you sure you're not sick? You feel feverish."

"It's not a fever. I run hot naturally." We reached the entrance to the cave, and I bounded over the edge and carried her inside, then helped her off my back.

"Jesus," she said, stumbling until her hand rested on the side of the cave. "I hope you know there is absolutely no chance of me free climbing down the way we came."

I laughed. "Don't worry. I've got you covered." I started ushering her inside but she stopped and dug her heels in.

"It's dark. Let me get my phone flashlight." She reached for her pocket.

I'd forgotten she couldn't see in the dark like I could. I placed a hand on hers. "No. Wait here. I'll light the fire."

I left her, breathing life back into my firepit and then

using a lit stick to ignite the sconces around the cave. I'd made it as comfortable as possible. A pile of furs worked as a bed, and a fresh spring formed a pool in the stone, serving as a bath. I had some chairs and a flat stone I was using as a table too. She'd need more than this as a human, but hopefully we wouldn't stay here long, not if she accepted me fully.

Reagan moved toward me from the cave's opening with wide, wondrous eyes. "Wow. How did you find this place?"

I approached her and started unzipping her coat, thinking about the most truthful way to answer that question without scaring her away. "My friends and I have been climbing here for years. It's good to have a shelter from the elements. I had similar places in Washington and Maine, but we were drawn back here recently."

Her lips parted. "Strange time of year for climbing and camping. I'm surprised your fingers didn't freeze."

The cave was already warming up thanks to the fire and my own dragon heat. I pushed the coat off her shoulders. "Care for a bath?"

She looked up at me, and I could see her mind working overtime. This was what I was afraid of. Reagan was curious to a fault and perceptive as a fox. Already I could sense her unease. Things weren't adding up, and she was trying to make sense of it all. I pinched her chin. "Don't."

"Don't what?"

"Ruin this by overthinking it." My dragon grew restless again, and before I could stop him, ordered, "Take off your clothes and get into the water."

Fuck me. That was a command. Reagan was a strong woman who valued her independence. I wasn't at all sure how she'd react to me bossing her around. Dragons could get in people's heads. We could manipulate dreams and push certain feelings to the surface. But I didn't want to manipulate Reagan. I wanted her to love me for me. I wanted her bonded to me so tightly that her human mind couldn't fathom ever being with anyone else. I wanted to ruin her for all other men.

Her eyes crinkled at the corners, and she reached for the hem of her sweatshirt. "Okay."

Hallelujah. She lifted the soft, heathery gray material over her head, revealing a pretty pink lace bra underneath. I wanted to bite through it with my teeth, but she stripped the bra off before I had the chance. Her boots were next, and then those damned leggings. I watched greedily as she unveiled flawless golden skin, ample curves, thick thighs, and breasts I desperately wanted to taste. I was hard in an instant, and just like that my dragon was in the driver's seat again.

"Beautiful," I rumbled. It was all my brain would supply.

Fuck. I was supposed to be telling her the truth, but my throat felt like charred coal from the heat growing in my chest. She shivered, and I held out my hand to her, pulling her back into my arms.

"God, you're so warm." She snuggled against me.

"Come." I led her toward the bath.

"It looks cold," she said, laughing.

I released her, reached behind my head and pulled off my sweater, then stripped out of my jeans. I entered the pool first. It was cold, but I channeled my inner fire into it, hoping she wouldn't notice the steam rising around me.

"Warm." I held out my hand to her.

She peered down at me, and I realized she was taking in my naked body through the clear water. She must have liked what she saw because she took my hand and stepped in.

"Oooh. Wow, it is warm." She smiled up at me. "What heats it? Is there something geothermal happening in these caverns?"

I didn't answer her. I couldn't without lying to her, and that was something I wouldn't do. She ran her hands up my chest, a move that made my inner beast stretch and arch against my skin to get closer to her.

"Holy mother of God," she mumbled under her breath. "It's like someone chiseled you from stone. How do you look like this? You're a barista, for God's sake. Do you work out constantly or something?"

I rumbled a laugh, running a hand up her back.

"No, really. You must know you're like ripped to shreds. How are you living in Thornsboro? Why aren't you in Hollywood, making millions as a male heart-throb?" She trailed her nails along my chest, around my ribs, up my back. "Seriously, Mason, what's your story?"

My curious cat had made an appearance again. She wanted answers, and I owed them to her. But first I had to wrestle my inner dragon into submission. He wanted her again and was making it impossible for me to keep my hands off her. I wanted to tell her everything. I wanted to explain. Instead, I brushed my fingers along the teeth marks on her neck where I'd claimed her and grunted, "*Mine.*"

"Yeah, you left a mark." A delicious blush stained her cheeks. "I guess we got a little rough. It doesn't hurt."

No. It would never hurt. The bite of a true mate only brought pleasure. My chest vibrated with my dragon's purr, and I planted a hand in the curve of her back and drew her tight against me. "Want you."

Her arms wrapped around my neck. "You sound like a caveman." Her eyes roved around the room. "Oh my god, you are a caveman! You have literally brought me back to your cave. Thank you for not clubbing me over the head." She laughed, and the sound was sweet music to my ears. I loved the sound of her laugh.

The hunger started again, gnawing at my belly, heating my blood. My balls felt heavy and my dick throbbed. I buried my hands in her hair and tipped her head. "Taste you?" I brought my mouth close to hers until our lips brushed.

"A-all right," she said softly.

Thank fuck. I'd tell her the truth. I would. Just as soon as I had more control.

I brushed her lips with mine, then kissed her properly, exploring her mouth with my tongue. She pulled me closer, until my cock was pressed between us. I needed more. I wrapped my hands around her waist and lifted her from the water, setting her bottom on the edge of the pool.

"What are you doing—?"

Lowering myself to hook her knees over my shoulders, I buried my face between her thighs, licking up her folds and flicking my tongue across her clit.

"Ohhh. Oh my god. Mason!" She leaned back on her elbows, staring down at me between the hard nipples of her breasts. I locked eyes with her as I licked inside, my tongue shifting partially to go deeper. She gasped and broke eye contact, her eyes rolling back with her head. Her hum of appreciation was all the encouragement I needed.

Seeing my mate take pleasure in what I was doing to her made my dragon purr. I settled in, studying what she liked, what made her squirm, what made her moan. I sucked and licked until my dragon knew the taste of her. And when her back finally arched off the stone with her cries of pleasure, the energy from her orgasm flowed into me through our bond. I'd heard that would happen once it was in place, but experiencing it was intense.

Her thighs shook and she collapsed onto her back, but I continued, teasing out the last dregs of her pleasure.

When she finally came down again, I lifted myself from the pool and gathered her into my arms. The stone here was two hard and cold for my human mate. My collection of furs near the fire would suit her better.

As I crossed the cave, she released her breath on a sigh, melting against me. "Mason... Wow." Her jaw worked. "That was... I don't have the words. I've never felt anything like that before. It's like we're connected."

"That's because we are." I stared down at her in my arms, knowing that she thought those words were some romantic notion a human man would say to a human woman. I needed to divest her of that misconception as soon as possible.

I lowered her into the soft nest of furs that served as my bed. Fed from the energy of her orgasm, my dragon had settled again, giving me a window of control. It was time. Time to show her exactly what I was and what it meant to be my mate. While I feared her rejection, I was more afraid of having to wipe her mind if that happened. But there was no stopping this mating. My dragon had chosen. Reagan was the one. And I could no longer fight the draw of the bond. This coupling was written in the stars, and I'd have to do my best to convince her to accept it.

I laid her down, spreading her bent knees and kneeling between her feet. She reached for me, her flushed cheeks and hooded eyes begging me to kiss her. "I want you in me," she whispered.

"Not yet. There's something I have to tell you. Before we do this again, I need you to know the truth about what I am."

Chapter Sixteen

REAGAN

Mason Forge was sex incarnate, and my body was perfectly ready to worship at his altar. I'd never orgasmed like I had twice that night. Both times it felt like my soul had left my body. I was still floating down from it even as my insides revved up for another go. Never before had it felt like this, but then I'd never been with a man like Mason.

He seemed to notice everything, down to the tiniest shift of my hips, and he'd react and give me exactly what I needed. Maybe it was because we had this connection, this thing I'd noticed between us lately, like the world stopped when our eyes met and all our gears met up and turned together. I'd thought it was only one-sided, this feeling, but I'd been wrong. I could see that Mason felt it too. However we'd ended up here, we were synced tonight, all our parts working in harmony, our souls locked in a dance that seemed predestined somehow.

"I think I know who you are, Mason. We've been talking for weeks."

"Not who I am. What I am." He seemed to struggle to find the words for what he was trying to tell me. The way he looked at me was like he was starving and I was his next meal. I'd never been wanted by a man to the point of his distraction. I wasn't *that* woman. No way would anyone call me sophisticated. I had an average build, complete with rolls around the middle, and although I could reasonably be called pretty, no one would fall off their bike trying to get a look at me. But lying there under this man, I felt truly beautiful. Truly wanted. The intensity of his gaze told me that in that moment, I was the center of his universe. With him, I was enough.

"Mason... I've never felt this level of... connection with anyone before," I said. "If you're going to tell me you're a crime boss on the lam, just do it, because I'm not sure there's anything you could say right now that would make me want to stop this from happening again." I was breathless. I propped myself up and reached for him, flattening my palm against his rock-hard abs.

He grabbed my wrist, closing his eyes and pressing his lips into a firm line. "Wait. Listen to me, okay?"

I returned my hand to the furs, resting back on both elbows. "Okay."

He sat on his heels. My god, his body was glorious. A tall, broad-shouldered tower of lean muscle, he had to be pushing six foot four, and that thing between his legs was large enough to be frightening. Hell, if he hadn't already been in me, there's no way I'd think it would fit.

"There's a reason you were able to find me tonight. A reason you feel a connection between us."

I nodded. "We've gotten to know each other these past weeks, better than I expected."

"More than that." He sighed heavily. "Reagan, you feel a connection because we *are* connected. You're my mate."

At first I thought he was joking or being overly dramatic, but the longer he kept staring at me, the more I realized he was serious. To Mason, *mate* had an actual meaning outside the possessive sense of the word. "All right," I drawled. "What does that mean to you?"

He licked his lips, and then my breath caught in my throat as two velvety black wings unfurled from his back. *Two. Actual. Fucking. Wings.*

I was on my feet and across the room, on the other side of the fire, before I'd even processed fully what was happening. Mason had wings. Mason had fucking WINGS! Growing out of his back! And if that wasn't terrifying enough, these weren't fluffy white angel wings. Oh no.

They were bat-like. Leathery. Framed in bone and amethyst scales. Each one had a talon as long as my forearm sprouting from its apex. Deadly, but undeniable beautiful.

My heart thundered in my chest. All I wanted to do was run, run, run. But where was I going to go? I ran toward the mouth of the cave, only for Mason to appear in front of me. He blocked the exit, his wings spanning the entire width of the opening.

Stopping my momentum was impossible, and I rammed right into his chest. Fuck. No wonder his body was too good to be true. It wasn't. He was some kind of... creature.

Experiment... My mind raced, trying to think of something that made sense.

"Shhh." He wrapped his arms around me and stroked my back.

I pushed against him and stumbled toward the fire, putting the blaze between us once more.

"I'm not going to hurt you. If I'd meant to hurt you, I could have done it several times over by now. In the woods. On the side of the mountain. By the tub." His voice grew low, husky.

Holding up a trembling hand, I tried to find my voice. *Focus on the story, Reagan.* "Wh-why do you have wings?"

He took a step toward me but stopped when I held my hand higher. "Because I'm a dragon."

What the actual fuck? Now I wasn't sure what to think. Was he insane? Confused? My mind couldn't absorb what he was saying alongside what I was seeing. Those wings had definitely come out of his back, and they were real, moving independently. "What do you mean by that? Is that some kind of code word for something, like how people in the Navy can be SEALs?"

Mason's brow arched and he laughed. "No. Not a code. I know this is a lot for you. Most humans don't know about our kind."

"Your kind?"

"We were sent here thousands of years ago by the great creator to help humans advance." He studied me, his hands landing on his hips when he saw my reaction to that comment. We were both still naked, and it was only now starting to make me uncomfortable. "You're cold. Put something on. This is a long story."

I reached down and grabbed what I thought was my gray sweatshirt off the floor. When I put it on, it fit me like a dress, and I realized it was his. The material was surprisingly soft and warm. I folded my arms and decided it would do.

"What about you?" I jutted my chin toward his nakedness.

"I'm fine. It's easier for me to be naked when I show you."

"Something more than the wings?" I asked incredulously.

He hung his head. "I don't want to scare you, Reagan, but I can see you don't believe me. It will be easier if I show you before I tell you more."

I waited expectantly. What happened next would stick with me until the day I died. Mason bent over, lifted his wings and... Oh my god. His limbs stretched and enlarged, purple scales shingling up his arms until they swallowed his protruding jaw. It all happened so quickly that I didn't even see his tail grow from the end of his spine until it appeared wrapped around his paws. Mason was a dragon! A vibrant purple-and-black, four-legged, prehistoric monster of a creature.

The spacious cavern suddenly seemed small and tight. I stumbled backward and had to catch myself on the cave wall.

The dragon's nose followed me, stopping only inches from my belly as I pressed my back against the smooth stone. I struggled to take a breath as he nuzzled my torsi and sniffed my neck. A gust of his breath blew back my hair. My chest hurt from the pounding of my heart. Jesus, his teeth were as long as my arm, and the atavistic rattle the beast was putting off reminded me of a rattlesnake. I trembled so hard my teeth clacked together. I cringed and he backed off, giving me space.

On some level I understood that I was looking at Mason, but my conscious mind couldn't accept it. All I felt was fear. And if the dragon's body hadn't been blocking the mouth of the cave, I would have thrown myself over the edge. I forced a swallow down a tight, breathless throat as tears streamed down my cheeks.

The dragon groaned and breathed out a deep sigh. The rattling stopped, and he lowered himself to his belly, chin to the cave floor. I waited for him to spring, to rip me to shreds or eat me in one bite. He didn't. Just watched me like a dog waiting for its master to give it a command.

I'm not sure how long I stood there. It had to have been an hour. I stared into the eyes of the dragon, and eventually my pulse slowed. Once I registered that this creature did not plan to have me for dinner, my muscles stopped shaking and the extra adrenaline flooding my system eased off to a mild, uncomfortable hum in my veins. I wiped my tears. My instinct to run morphed into a general anxiety that eventually vanished altogether.

Although larger and set in the head of a horrific monster, the eyes of the beast were still Mason's. The way he was looking at me tugged something deep within my heart. He wanted my acceptance, and he was holding painfully still to get it.

I read somewhere that the human body has three typical reactions to a terrifying stimulus. Alongside mental disorganization, the nervous system goes haywire and our instincts tell us fight, flight, or fawn. Fight never crossed my mind. Who in their right mind would try to fight a dragon with nothing but his shirt on her back? Flight, I might have tried if it didn't mean hurling myself to my death. It wasn't an option anyway with him blocking the exit. Which left fawning.

I'd fawned. I'd gone perfectly still, and eventually I'd realized there was nothing to be afraid of. But that's not where our fear response ends. People enjoy roller coasters and horror movies because afterward, when we know we're safe, we experience something called the excitation transfer response. Our brains and bodies remain exhilarated even when the fear has passed.

That's what I felt as I reached out toward the dragon. All the razor's-edge excitement of the moment before, transferred into a kind of wonder. Oh, my hands still shook as I neared the creature, but when my fingers met the ridges of his face, I was fascinated. The dragon closed his eyes and made a deep, throaty purr. I traced over one of his horns, then along the shingled scales of his neck and back. I spent a few minutes examining the bony protrusion that patterned his tail. I poked a talon jutting from one of its massive paws with my finger and leaped back when the paw jerked toward his body, his head moving to see what I was doing.

He rolled partway onto his back, and I circled my hand on his belly like he was the world's biggest dog. Those enormous blue eyes rolled back in his head. He was enjoying this.

Folding my arms, I took a step back. "Does this transformation go both ways? Because I think we're going to have a hard time talking about this with you..." I circled a hand to indicate his current state of monsterhood.

The dragon's lips pulled back from his teeth, and fear flooded me again... until I realized he was smiling. I backed up another step as his scales tipped up, his wings folded in, and his body turned, shrinking, changing. It was a quick, efficient process, and when it was done, Mason stood before me again, painfully nervous.

"I didn't mean to scare you," he said softly. "There was no other way to get you to truly understand."

I swallowed. "Is that what this is? Understanding? I feel as confused as ever." I rubbed my palms together in circles between us. "You're a dragon." Fuck, it still sounded ridiculous.

"Yes."

"You said something about you and your friends coming here before. You're not the only one then?"

He gestured for me to sit down, rubbing the back of

his neck. I lowered myself onto the furs and he knelt in front of me. "How about a drink?"

"How about you give me some answers?" As much as I'd love to numb what I was feeling with alcohol, I wanted to know the truth more.

"Thousands of years ago, the great creator sent my kind to Earth from the stars to help humans evolve from creatures living as animals to what you are today. We... Dragons... We have a symbiotic relationship with your kind." His voice took on a resonance as he explained, a hollow quality that gave me chills.

"Whoa. Wait a minute. Are you saying you've lived among us from the beginning of our history, but somehow no one knows you exist?" I shook my head.

He ran his finger along the fur. "Some people know, but the truth is we work hard to keep our existence secret. We look like you. We live among you. But our presence puts off energy that inspires you. Every major human accomplishment has been inspired by dragons." He gestured toward me. "You said it yourself, every time you came into the café and spent time with me, you had an epiphany that moved you forward toward your goal."

I lowered my chin. "What? Are you suggesting that you are, quite literally, a muse?"

He slanted me a half grin. "No. I'm telling you I am a dragon, but we have the same qualities as the legends you call muses." He moved closer to me, and I was overcome with a keen awareness that he was naked and I was engulfed in his sweater. "Before I tell you anymore, you have to promise me never to share any of this."

I gazed up at him, feeling his worry deep within my soul. This was his secret, and it was a big one. As a journalist though, I lived to report the truth. "I don't understand. Why is this a secret at all? If you're helping people and not hurting anyone, why not go public?"

He sighed, his shoulders slumping as he looked toward the place his fingers drew nervous patterns in the fur. "Because the secret society you've been researching... the Saint's Order? I know their purpose, Reagan. I can tell you exactly what that gathering is about without you ever having to set foot in Harpers Ferry."

A chill raced through me.

"They're a society sworn to kill and control dragons."

Chapter Seventeen

MASON

Reagan's expression was unreadable, but at least she wasn't trying to throw herself from the mouth of the cave anymore. Not that I thought she'd do that. She was too smart to take such a foolhardy action. But her intelligence was what I was worried about now.

I'd never met a human as curious as Reagan. It was why she was a natural at her profession. But while she might be a regular Lois Lane, I couldn't be her Superman. Superman was one person, and he was able to keep his true identity a secret. Reagan knew who I was and where I lived, and if she told the world about me, it would negatively affect thousands of dragons.

She held up her hands. "Stop. Why would the Saint's Order want to kill you?"

"Think about who their members are." As I spoke, I walked over to my bag and pulled on a pair of gray joggers. I wasn't sure if my nudity was making her uncomfortable, but it seemed like the polite thing to do considering she was wearing my sweater. I still wanted to fuck her. My mating sickness was hardly satisfied, and my dragon was already urging me to get her naked again. But I wouldn't do that without her knowing everything. It was the only way to make her my true mate.

"They're the rich and powerful. Senators, Supreme Court justices, billionaire business owners, celebrities." She shrugged.

"Exactly. People on top don't like innovation unless it directly benefits them. They only want what they can own, control, or force upon you. Dragons are a threat to them because we bring disruption. We don't favor the rich. Anyone who comes near us could be inspired to completely transform an industry or bring about a revolution."

"You represent risk to the status quo," she said softly.

"Yes. And the thing the superrich fear the most is not being rich anymore. When Saint George slayed one of our kind, it wasn't because the dragon was eating women and children as history suggests. It was because a woman, a princess, was inspired by the dragon to challenge the patriarchal religious leaders of the time and started to gather followers to her cause. Saint George learned the truth about the dragon's nature, slaughtered him, and married off the princess. That's what started the war."

"The war?"

"Between the Saint's Order and the Zodiac Brotherhood, our warrior class."

She leaned back on her elbows, staring up at the ceiling of the cave. "Okay, I'm not even going to pretend I remember the details behind Saint George slaying a dragon, but I think we'd all know if there was a war going on between a bunch of dragons and a bunch of wealthy elites."

I rubbed the back of my neck again, wincing as I unloaded the next bit of news. "You do know. You call it the crusades. Have you ever wondered why the Knights Templar wore the cross of Saint George? What brought about the Renaissance? The Age of Enlightenment? We were there. Dragons were the match that started the fire of every great advancement of man and the Order's backlash against it. We protect ourselves when they retaliate."

Her eyes narrowed. "What about now? If you're at war, why can't we see it now?"

"After the last world war, things were dire for us. We'd lost so many lives. A powerful and selfless member of our warrior class, a Libra named Donovan, sacrificed himself to the Order in exchange for a peace accord. He's their permanent prisoner now. He stays voluntarily in exchange for a moratorium on hunting us, and they use him for his power."

Reagan crisscrossed her legs and leaned toward me with that glint in her eye like she was onto something. "But then why is the Order growing? If their purpose was to kill dragons, and Donovan made it so that they can't do that anymore, then why even have an Order anymore?"

I snorted. "Good question. It's because the terms of our agreement state that if an Order member can catch one of us on their land, they can keep us. Owning one of us, like they own Donovan, is these people's wet dream, Reagan. Imagine the power of creativity you could unleash on your staff if you had a dragon as your prisoner, and everything they'd produce using that celestial energy would be owned and controlled by you. It's a perversion of our purpose. Luckily, it rarely happens. But there's enough captured dragons that the Saint's Order can continue their secret endeavors, passing down the knowledge of how to use and kill dragons from father to son."

"Jesus."

"Yeah." I move closer to her, crisscrossing my own legs so that we're knee to knee. "There's something else." This was the part that had to do with her, and I prayed to the creator that she wouldn't freak about it. "Dragons who don't mate regenerate after about a hundred years. The ones they capture eventually go back to the creator. And when that happens, the Saint's Order tries to trick a dragon into making a mistake. They need replacements."

"You believe in reincarnation."

I nodded. "Our mating sickness—we call it appetency—gets worse and worse until we eventually go up in flames, and yes, we believe we are reborn."

Her breath hitched. "That's how you were sick, isn't it? You have mating sickness."

She said the last part slowly, as if it was just sinking in. "What happens to dragons who mate?"

"We live incredibly long lives, as do our mates."

"How long?" Her green eyes spark with curiosity.

"It varies, just like with humans, but on average nine hundred years give or take. Our Oracle and her mate are thousands of years old."

"Jesus," she said breathlessly. "Wait, you called *me* your mate."

I leaned in close and looked her directly in the eye. "I did... *mate*."

Chapter Eighteen

REAGAN

Mate. This time when he said it and I was looking straight into his face, I picked up on things I hadn't before. From the intensity of his gaze to the way his jaw grew tight, his expression loaded the word with meaning. He might as well have said I was his wife. Only this word seemed more somehow. "Mate... like an animal's mate?"

He inclined his head. "A dragon's mate."

Holy. Fucking. Shit. "What exactly does that word mean to you, Mason?" I asked breathlessly.

"You mean what does it mean to us? You're as affected as I am or you wouldn't have come here. You wouldn't have been able to find me. That pull in your chest, that connection you told me about that moved you, that was the mating call. That was the dragon inside you calling out to the one inside me."

I laughed. I couldn't help it. "I hate to disappoint you, but there is no dragon inside me. I mean, I get grumpy before my morning coffee, but I have never sprouted wings." I pointed to the space where his wings had been.

"No," he said in a voice so low it sounded as if he'd dragged it across the floor of the cave. "You aren't a dragon, but you do have dragon blood in your DNA. Many people do, actually. We've intermixed over the centuries, although most of the time it remains dormant. Some has to be there though, or you wouldn't have felt the bond."

I spread my hands. "It was a lucky guess, Mason. I saw the photograph hanging on your wall and I had a hunch."

A ghost of a smile turned the corners of his lips. "Lucky?" He gave a low chuckle. "I'd say that's almost miraculous. Improbable. Implausible." He glanced down at our touching knees, his sweater pulled taut between my thighs and just barely covering what was between them.

I swallowed. "It is what it is."

"You accepted me as your mate in the woods. I claimed you." He spoke slowly, as if talking to a small child. The timbre of his voice made my heart stutter.

"I... I had sex with you. That's all. We've been flirting. We're both adults. It's natural." I wasn't sure why I was fighting him so hard on this mate thing except that it didn't seem to be just a label. It seemed to mean something deeper, bigger, more permanent, and I wasn't ready for that. How could I be? We'd never even been on an official first date.

His eyes narrowed, the muscles in his jaw popping like he wanted to say something that he was holding back. "There's a way we can test the mating bond. Know for sure if it's in place."

"How?" The way he was looking at me made my heart skitter, and a zing traveled to places low within me. My nervous system was suddenly on high alert.

His eyes met mine and the purr came back. Ah, the sound was something I could feel. It buzzed pleasantly against my skin even as it soothed my nerves. My breath quickened. I shifted my legs and feet to one side so I could clench my thighs together against the ache forming between them.

"Reagan," he cooed, and oh my god, heat bloomed between my legs just hearing my name on his lips. "Let me see you. Take off the sweater."

I licked my lips, my body thrumming as if I were a violin whose strings he'd plucked. The sweater was over my head, gripped between my hands before I even thought to do it. He hadn't made me do it, but at his suggestion, I wanted it off desperately. My skin sang for his touch. That purr. God, I just wanted him to touch me.

"Mason, I... I need." I rubbed the space over my heart.

"Yeah. I'll give you what you need. Lie back."

I did, my knees spreading. I was completely naked, spread out before him like a banquet, and I wasn't the least bit shy or ashamed. Like before, it just felt right, like we were in sync, dancing to the same song. He removed his pants and knelt between my feet, the proud length of him jutting over my lower body. I propped myself on an elbow and ran my nails down his abs until I reached the base of his shaft. My hand stroked the length of him, covering him in the wetness that wept from the tip.

He closed his eyes and hummed, running his hands along my inner thighs. "Are you ready for me, mate?"

He ran a knuckle along my slit. I was soaked, and he growled his appreciation.

"Yes," I breathed. "I need you in me." Half-crazed with desire, I arched my back to bring my core closer to him, and he pressed a hand into my chest, sliding it up to loosely grip my throat just under my jaw. Held like that, I was at his mercy, but I just whimpered for more.

"Shhh, I've got you." The head of his massive cock pressed against my opening and started to slowly penetrate me. I was a little sore from the woods, and if anything, he felt bigger than before, stretching me until the sheer size of him stopped his progression. I took a deep breath as he retreated marginally before sinking in deeper and gaining some ground.

I arched and wrapped my legs around his hips, drawing him down until he was entirely inside me. He paused, his hand still around my throat, his weight braced on a single elbow near my head. He looked down at me, looked into my eyes, his wings unraveling, spreading above us.

"You can feel it, can't you?" he whispered.

I tried to grind against him, but he held firm. "Of

course I can feel you. You're so deep inside me I can taste you in my throat."

"You can feel my mating trill."

"The purr? Feel it. Hear it. Oh my god, it's like my entire body is vibrating with it." I closed my eyes and tipped my head back, arching against him again and grinding myself as hard as possible. I wanted him to move. I wanted him to fuck me. I was desperate for friction, for sensation.

A smile spread across his face, and he pulled out only to slam into me again. "Reagan, a dragon's mating trill can only be heard and felt by one's mate. To others, it's completely silent."

I thought he was joking at first. Surely anyone within earshot could hear the vibration coming from Mason's chest. But then I closed my eyes and tried to pinpoint exactly where the sound was coming from and realized I couldn't. It was in the air. It was rumbling between us. Oh my god, maybe it was coming from inside me.

Concentrating on it made the heat bloom between my legs again, and I slipped my fingers into the back of his hair. "Please, Mason. Please, please, please,"

He thrust again and I groaned. "A dragon male can make their mate orgasm with a single command." His hips increased their pace, his thrusts hitting me in just the right spot but without the intensity as before.

I writhed beneath him. Frantically, I dug my nails into his ass. "More. Mason, I need—"

"Are you my mate, Reagan?" he gritted out through clenched teeth.

Shit. Admitting that I was his mate meant believing in a bond that was far more serious than I was ready for but not admitting it would be denying what was right in front of me. I heard it all around me, in his trill, in his voice. Proof of it hummed against my skin. I tasted it on his kiss. The scent of it filled my lungs. I was drowning in proof that he was my mate, and worse, I didn't want to come up for air.

With a beat of his wings, we rose from the furs, and I desperately wrapped my legs and arms around him, afraid I might fall. We lifted into the air. In this position, all my weight settled on the place where our bodies joined. Every beat of his wings drove him deeper. I was close. So very close.

"Oh God, Mason!"

We reached the ceiling of the cave, and he hooked his wings into the rock, grabbed me by the waist and the back of the head. Suspended, swinging above the cave, my body warred between fear and ecstasy. I'd lost all control, but the pleasure was like nothing I'd felt before. I was a supernova, a hairbreadth from exploding.

"Mason, please. God, I'm so close."

"Are you my mate?" he demanded again.

I couldn't hold back. Not anymore. "Yes!" I cried. "I'm your mate."

"Then come for me, baby."

I didn't so much hear his voice as feel it like a warm, wet lick of energy from the tips of my toes to the top of my head. I came so hard my teeth clacked together and I arched in his arms, my lids fluttering closed as my internal wiring blew apart and then rearranged itself again. The pleasure was intense enough I lost my grip on him.

But he had me. In the throes of my orgasm, he released his hold on the ceiling, and we dropped. His wings caught air, and he lowered us to the furs. As soon as we touched down, he unleashed himself on me, hammering into me even as my inner walls spasmed around him. With a roar loud enough to shake the cave walls, he came apart, his orgasm triggering another from me.

And I knew. I knew it was true. He was my mate. I still wasn't sure all that came with the title, but I accepted it like I accepted the sun would rise in the morning. I didn't realize then what a gift a sunrise was, what a gift it would become, but I knew, without a doubt, I was Mason Forge's mate.

I'd never deny it again.

Chapter Nineteen

MASON

Once I'd helped Reagan clean up, I tucked both of us between the furs and wrapped her in my wings. She rested her head on my chest, her eyelids growing heavy and her breath evening out. Watching her fall asleep proved almost as enjoyable as tiring her out. My dragon's protective instincts were finally appeased with her in my arms. I ran a hand over her hair, wrapped a golden strand around my finger.

"It would be so easy to love you," she whispered as she drifted off.

I brushed my lips across her temple. I already loved her. She was mine and always would be. I didn't blame her for taking longer to realize she loved me too. This bond was new to both of us, and I'd heard it took longer for her kind to form an attachment. I'd wait as long as necessary for her to come to understand her feelings.

Content at last, the pain of mating sickness now a distant memory, I slept.

I woke to someone shaking my shoulder, my lungs filled with vanilla and lavender. My face was buried in blond fluff, my arms wrapped around Reagan's sleeping body. Slowly I opened my eyes and saw Andromeda standing over me in nothing but a nightgown, her wings out.

"Andy?" I whispered.

"Sorry to bother you. I need your help. Alex is in my cave and won't leave. He's totally having a meltdown. He drank way too much last night and is absolutely inconsolable." She sighed.

"I would, it's just..." I kept my voice low, not wanting to wake Reagan, but when I turned to look at Andy, my wing pulled back from my mate's face.

"Oh my god," Andy squealed, her knuckles going to her lips. "Is that her? Is that your mate? I thought you said—"

"Shhh!" I pressed a finger to my lips and slowly extricated myself from Reagan, tucking the furs around her. Carefully, I got up and pulled on my pants. Andy had seen me naked dozens of times—every time we shifted— but that was a necessity. This wasn't. And I didn't want my mate to see me and get the wrong idea or suffer any jealousy. I walked Andy toward the mouth of the cave, noticing the sky had taken on a silvery quality. The sun was rising.

"Reagan came to me last night," I explained. "Hers was the scream we heard."

"I'd wondered when you left so quickly." Andy gripped my shoulders. "You have to go to the Oracle and ask for her blessing."

"I plan to. I'll take her home today and then make the arrangements."

"Who is this?" Reagan said from behind me. I turned to see that she was up, dressed, and glaring daggers at Andy.

I barely contained my laugh. "This is my friend Andy, Reagan. She's another Pisces dragon."

Reagan strode forward until she was slightly in front of me and folded her arms over her chest. "Nice to meet you." It sounded a lot like *fuck off*.

"It's good to meet you too, Reagan. Anytime a friend finds a mate, it's reason to celebrate."

"Wait, is this cappuccino-foam-art Andy?" Reagan shifted uneasily, and I couldn't help but preen a little over the jealousy wafting off her.

Andy's eyes flicked up to mine and then back to Reagan. "He told you about that?"

Reagan's face contorted in a poorly disguised scowl. "What brings you by so early?"

"You know what? Nothing. I-I'm sorry to disturb you." Andy spread her red wings and turned toward the cave mouth.

"Wait!" I took Reagan by the shoulders and turned her to face me, loving the way she seemed to want to block me from Andy's view. "Andy asked for my help dealing with a male who won't leave her cave. He's dangerous. Can you wait here with her while I go and handle him?" I made it clear that Andy would be staying with her, not coming with me. Reagan didn't understand the power behind what she was feeling right now, but had I left with Andy at that moment, it would have torn her in two.

"How dangerous?" she asked, placing her hands on my bare chest.

No one had ever looked at me the way she did just then, as if I were the sun, and if anything ever happened to me, there would be no light in her world. I couldn't see the expression on my own face, but in my heart, I felt the same way.

I gave her a reassuring smile. The last thing I wanted was for her to worry about me. "Trust me, I can handle Alex. This won't take long."

Reluctantly, she nodded her head. "Only if you're sure you'll be safe."

I kissed her forehead. "I will be. Alex is an asshole but not a killer." I passed Andy on the way to the edge, murmuring, "Take care of her. I'll be right back."

Chapter Twenty

REAGAN

I was losing my damn mind. As Mason spread his dark wings and leaped off the side of the cliff to fly to God knows where, I was not at all concerned that dragon-shifting people existed in my world or that I'd had unprotected sex with a man I'd known for a matter of weeks. Nope, every fiber of my being was obsessively tracking the gorgeous, winged woman beside me for any indication she might challenge me for my mate. I was jealous that she'd known him before I did. I was jealous she had wings and I didn't. My teeth were grinding at her pretty red hair and slender figure.

"I owe you an apology, Andy," I said because I'd never felt like such an asshole before. I was a logical human being. I refused to act on the emotional impulses teeming inside my body.

"Why?" she asked with a small laugh. "I was the one that interrupted your morning."

"Because... I'm not sure what's happening to me, but I sort of want to fight you right now, and I don't know why." I took a deep breath and blew it out slowly.

She laughed from deep in her belly. "It's natural. You're newly mated. Stars, you're handling it really well actually."

"I'm glad you think so, because I need to ask you for a favor."

"What?"

"Can you fly me down to the bathrooms? Mason took me last night, but it's been like nine hours."

"Oh, of course!"

Before I could say another word, Andy swept me into her arms, proving that she was stronger than she looked. It was a good thing I hadn't acted on my desire to attack her because I would have ended up on my ass. She flew me down to the cinderblock public restroom I'd used the night before.

"I forgot my coat," I said, shivering the moment she set me down.

"I'll warm it up for you."

She followed me inside, waiting by the sinks while I went into one of the stalls. In moments, it was warm enough for my teeth to stop chattering.

"Thanks." I finished and washed my hands at the sink beside her.

"Don't mention it." She gave me a knowing smile. "I'm just incredibly happy for you and Mason. He deserves a true mate. Do you mind if I ask when your birthday is?"

"December twenty-second. Why?"

She pressed a finger into her chin in a way I found disturbingly charming. Why couldn't she look like an ogre and have the personality of a rabid Chihuahua? "A Capricorn. It's auspicious. The Oracle will know if you're truly compatible, but I think your chances are excellent."

"Chances of what?" I frowned. I didn't like the sound of that. Why would someone else's opinion have anything to do with our chances as a couple?

"Being happy together and true to each other. She sees the future. You're human, so she'll have to approve your mating and human marriage. Didn't Mason tell you?"

"No." I dried my hands and glanced at my feet. Marriage was the last thing on my mind. This relationship was intense and passionate, but we were both young. We had years to think about marriage. "We didn't get that far. It's so new."

"Sorry," she said, grimacing.

"No. Thanks for giving me a heads-up. I'm sure that might be an issue someday." I moved past her for the door.

I heard her groan, and when I turned my head to look back at her, my hand poised on the door handle, I noticed she'd squeezed her eyes shut.

"There's just one more thing," she said.

Whatever it was, it looked like it was giving her a headache. My body clenched at the way she looked at me, and I braced myself for her to admit she was in love with him. That was my guess based on the look in her eyes.

"Well?" I prompted. It wasn't like I could climb back up to Mason's cave, so I was anxious to listen to what she had to say and have her return me to him as soon as possible.

"Mason and I have been friends since we were children," she said. "He's like a brother to me. I care about him deeply."

"Okay." I liked the part about him being like a brother. Not so much about the caring.

"He told me you're a journalist."

What? He talked to her about my job? I bristled. "I would never say anything about dragons' existence. I promised him I wouldn't, and frankly, no one would believe it anyway without one of you coming forward and revealing yourself."

"Right, but... the Order." She tucked her hair behind her ear, hesitating, searching for the right words.

I wasn't going to promise that I wouldn't report on the Saint's Order. No one needed to know the secret society's relationship to dragons. "I think this is probably something I should discuss with Mason."

She looked down at her feet. "All I ask is that you don't do anything to hurt him, Reagan. You're both vulnerable right now."

She didn't elaborate on what she meant by that, and I didn't ask her to. Instead, I gave her a reassuring smile. I had no intention of doing anything that would endanger

Mason. Even the thought made me weirdly unsettled. But I also had no intention of backing off my goal of exposing the Order. "I'd never intentionally hurt Mason."

"Good." She sighed. "I like you already. I hope we can become close friends."

As much as I'd wanted to kill her only moments ago, I had to give her props for being a good friend to Mason. "Well, we're already going to the bathroom together."

She laughed.

By the time she flew me back up to the cave, Mason was already waiting for us and pulled me into his arms as if he hadn't seen me in a month. As crazy as it was, I loved the attention and the possessiveness. I already wanted him again.

"Alex is gone," he said to Andy.

"Did you hurt him?"

Mason smiled. "Probably not enough to keep him from trying again tomorrow night."

She sighed. "Thanks. I'll figure something out since you'll be gone."

I stared up at Mason. "You're coming back to Thornsboro early?"

He grinned. "I don't need to be here anymore now that I've claimed you."

"Oh." All the pieces fit together. "You don't have mating sickness anymore because we..." I hooked my fingers together.

He ducked his chin in affirmation.

I glanced back at Andy, concerned for her. If this was a group of dragons suffering from mating sickness, I could only imagine how much unwanted attention she must get. "Are you sure you'll be okay here?"

She smirked. "Safer for me to be here than among humans. Later, Mason. Nice to meet you, Reagan." She pushed off the edge of the cave and flew off.

Mason handed me my coat and mittens. "Let's get you home."

Chapter Twenty-One

REAGAN

Although I would have loved to take Mason up on his offer to go back to his apartment and continue where we'd left off, I needed to get home to walk and feed Litz. I also needed to face my father. For the first time ever, I'd stayed out all night without clearing it with him first. I knew he'd be furious, and I didn't want to introduce him to Mason under the circumstances. My phone was dead—an unfortunate side effect of spending the night in a cave—but he'd probably been trying to text or call all night. I braced myself for an angry tirade as I walked through the mudroom from the garage, my footstep echoing on the marble floor of the two-story foyer.

Carlotta passed me with a vacuum in her hand. "Good morning, Ms. Reagan. I walked and fed Litz for you since I noticed you had an early morning."

Early morning? "Oh, you didn't have to do that. Thank you."

"You're welcome." Not a hint of worry marred her smile. Did she even suspect I'd been out all night?

"Has Dad left for the office yet?"

"I don't think so. He's still upstairs." She lowered her voice. "And in a rare good mood!" She went about her work, singing softly.

I padded up the stairs. Dad in a good mood... I hadn't seen that in a while. Litz bolted out of my room when I opened the door, butting my knees with his head. I gave him some cuddles. Was it possible my overnight absence had gone unnoticed? Smiling to myself, I showered and changed. When I came out of my room, dressed and ready for the office, Dad was standing in the hall.

"Reagan, I'm glad you're finally up! Can I speak with you for a moment?"

Finally up? Oh my god, he *hadn't* noticed. I tried not to take that personally. He was a busy man and I was an adult. It wasn't like he read me a story and tucked me in every night. Plus, I was overwhelmingly relieved to not have to face his wrath about it. So why did it hurt a little that my only parent hadn't even realized I was missing?

"Yeah. Actually, I have some news myself."

He tilted his head toward his office, and I followed him inside. The room gave me parochial school library vibes that day, and I caught myself trying to be quiet even though there was no one there to hold a finger to their lips. It felt like walking into a church or a funeral home.

He took a seat behind the desk, and I lowered myself into the chair across from him. Clasping his hands together in front of him he said, "We got the contract."

I sat up straighter. "The school-lunch contract? That's great! That's fabulous. Congratulations!"

"It's bigger than I ever dreamed, Reagan, and now that I'm on the other side of it, I think I owe you an apology."

My mouth dropped open. I'd never expected to hear those words come out of my father's mouth. I tried to think of something to say but ended up making a noise like "Oh?"

"I think the stress of this deal led me to grow impatient with you. I wanted your help. I needed someone inside Bailey that I could trust, so I tried to pressure you into coming to work for me. I'm sorry about that. You don't need to move out or quit your job."

I took a deep breath. I believed he meant every word, but I also believed that we'd never be right until I flew the nest. "Thanks for that, but I found a place in town, and I think it's time I stood on my own two feet."

Dad's smile faltered. "No, Peanut. I'd like you to stay. You don't have to move out."

I chewed my lip. "I think it would be better for us if I did though. You were right when you said I don't know what it's like to be on my own. I think it's time I found out. The last thing I want is for you to come to resent me for not working at Bailey while I benefit from the hard work you do. This way, with my own place, we can both appreciate each other in a new light, plan time together, get to know each other again."

His eyes grew misty. "I don't want you to go."

Part of me wanted to promise I'd stay, just to make him happy. But I knew he'd never view me as an adult until I started acting like one. "It's time, Dad. It'll be okay. You'll see." He nodded. "All right then. It sounds like you've made your decision."

"I have."

"I do have one request."

"What's that?"

"I'm being honored at an event on Friday for my accomplishments at Bailey. I was hoping you could be my guest, considering your mother..."

My heart squeezed at the look in his eyes. I was his only family, the only one to cheer him on for any award he might receive. But going with my dad to his event meant I couldn't follow up on the Saint's Order initiation in Harpers Ferry. Mason would be happy about that, and after what Andy told me, I wasn't sure I should go anyway. Still, deep in my heart, I felt a dream start to die like a rose sagging on the vine. I wanted that story. I still thought there was a way I could have Mason and expose the Saint's Order, maybe it just couldn't involve Harper's Ferry.

"I'd love to go, Dad."

He stood and rounded the desk, pulling me out of the chair and into his arms. "Thank you, Peanut." He kissed the side of my head.

Afterward, I walked toward my room, feeling torn.

Was I giving up on my dream by choosing Mason and my father over the story? I'd always had this drive, a fire in me to accomplish whatever I set out to do. I was tempted to turn around and tell my father I couldn't go with him.

No. I shook my head, resolved to let this one go. I had time. There would be other opportunities. Dad needed me, and I couldn't risk hurting Mason. I tried to feel good about the decision, and then I tried not to think about it at all.

Chapter Twenty-Two

MASON

"I ordered a vanilla latte." The man across the counter from me scowled at the dirty chai I was trying to shove in front of him.

"Sorry," I mumbled. I swept it into the sink and turned back to the espresso machine to make him his actual order. I'd been like this all day, unable to concentrate.

I'd wanted Reagan to stay with me after our time in Smoke Hole Canyon, but it was a weekday and she'd needed to face her father and get back to work. So did I. I reopened Forge's and had been fielding questions about my absence all day. The town was small, and it seemed like half the population was in my café, trying to get the scoop on why I'd left and then returned before the date on my note. I wasn't giving them anything, which was pure fodder for the gossip mill.

"I heard he was supposed to get married but his bride left him at the altar," a woman whispered at a table behind me. I snorted. That was a good one.

"Well, I heard he's in the witness-protection program and had to go into hiding for a few days," another one said.

The buzz behind me continued as I finished the man's latte and set it in front of him. "Here you are. Sorry for the confusion."

He grunted and looked back at his phone.

Although I was relieved not to be suffering from appetency any longer, working at Forge's that day was almost painful. All I could think about was how many hours were left until Reagan walked through my door. How many minutes until I could get her home? How many seconds before I could bury myself inside her? My dragon refused to think about anything else, and I grew increasingly agitated as the clock counted down.

My phone rang, and by the ring tone I knew it was Uncle Connor. I ducked into the back room and answered. "I can't talk long. Business is booming."

"I'll make this quick then. A little dragon told me you mated the journalist."

Damn it, Andy! "Yeah. She came to me, Connor. It just happened. I had no control once she put herself in my path and told me she was willing."

He gave a low laugh. "Of course not. You did everything you could." The connection went silent for a beat. "What was it like?"

Connor had never had a mate, and I tried to think of

ways to describe it. "Remember that time when I was little and you were watching me for Mom? We did a puzzle together and when we finished it, there was one piece missing."

"Yeah, frustrating as hell."

"Finding my mate was a lot like when we found that last piece in the carpet and slipped it into the open spot. I finally felt complete."

"Damn." Connor went silent on the other end of the line. "Then I feel a little bad relaying the message I have for you."

"What message?"

"You need to come to Cardinal Island."

"I was planning on it... to get the Oracle's blessing on my mating Reagan."

"This isn't about that, Mason. After training last night, the Oracle asked to speak with you. I think it's about the brotherhood." There was a pause. "You didn't hear this from me, but there's a rumor that Solomon might step down to spend more time with his young."

Raw jubilation flooded my system. I'd known since the day I was born that I had warrior blood. How could I not, being my father's son and having an uncle on my mother's side who was also a warrior? But there were hundreds of warrior-class dragons in the world. The Oracle called only twelve of them to be brothers, and once in that position, the men who served rarely stepped down.

"I don't know what to say. I'll be there. Should I bring Reagan?"

"Not yet. Not without permission. Sorry, man. You know the rules."

"Right. Right. It will be hard to breathe without her near me, but if the Oracle wants to see me, I'll be there."

"Right. See you Friday."

Once we said our goodbyes, I slipped back behind the counter, still vibrating with excitement over the possibility of becoming a brother. The place had cleared out in the time it took to talk to Connor. Even the man at the counter had gone, leaving me a decent tip which was surprising given I'd initially served him the wrong drink. I glanced at my watch. Almost six o'clock; Reagan must be working late. Alone in the coffee shop, I watched out the window as the sky beyond darkened.

The bell above the door chimed and my life walked in, smiling as though she'd slept more than three hours last night. I leaped over the counter and met her halfway, twirling her in my arms and giving her a firm kiss.

"Wow, you really know how to say hello to a girl."

She melted against me, her green eyes warming in a way I found irresistible. She was smaller than me in every way. Tiny, even though by human standards she'd be called curvy. But when Reagan wanted something, she went for it. She climbed my body, hoisting herself up by my hips and shoulders, and kissed me like she needed my mouth to breathe. I kissed her back but kept one eye on the door. Forge's was still open, and the last thing I wanted was someone seeing us like this in a gossipy small town like Thornsboro.

Once she slid off me, I offered to make her drink,

adjusting myself in my pants and keeping a tight leash on my inner dragon. "How did things go with your father this morning?"

Her eyes danced and her lips twitched like she was still trying to make sense of it. "Fine. He didn't even notice I'd been out all night. Actually, he apologized for before and offered to let me stay."

"Are you going to?"

"No. I'm going to lease the Whitman place. I think it's time."

I turned that over in my mind. I wanted her to live with me, but something told me I should wait to ask her. Give her time to get used to our mating.

"He asked me to be his guest at some kind of award ceremony Friday."

I grabbed her special red cup off the stack and started her cappuccino. "So does that mean you won't be pursuing the Saint's Order gathering?" I asked with obvious relief.

She fidgeted on her stool. "Andy told me I shouldn't go, and now I have this thing with my father. To be honest, Mason, it feels like I'm giving up on my dreams for the men in my life, and I don't like it. I'd never report on your secret. But their secret... the society's... they need to be outed."

I concentrated on her cup as I poured a perfect heart in her foam. "Andy told you not to go, huh? Did she explain why?"

"Not really."

I slid her cup in front of her and leaned my elbows on

the counter. "The dragon I showed you last night is me... and it isn't. He's a part of me, one that is ruled more by instinct and celestial energy than logical thought." I rubbed my forehead. "No. That's not entirely true. He's intelligent and logical, just not when it comes to you."

"Okay." She laughed.

"To my dragon, you are the highest priority. You are to me as well, but I have the capacity to decide. Understand?"

She shook her head. "Not at all."

I sighed. How to explain...? "Say you wanted to go bungee jumping. I might think that was dangerous and ask you not to do it. But if you really wanted to go anyway, I could close my eyes and force myself not to interfere." I let that sink in for a beat.

Her eyes widened. "Your dragon can't."

I shook my head. "Nope. He'd catch you. It would be the most boring bungee jump in history."

A giggle escaped her lips. "Thank God I'm not an adrenaline junkie."

"You might not think of it as risky, but you going to where the Saint's Order is registers as just as dangerous to my dragon, especially now, during my alignment. If I knew you were going, I wouldn't be capable of letting you go alone. And if I set foot on Order grounds, they have a right to capture or hunt me, Reagan. I'm being honest when I say I'm not sure I could keep myself from coming for you. My father couldn't when it was my mother in their clutches."

Thinking about my father caused my muscles to

tense and I straightened, distracting myself by cleaning up my workspace.

"Your mother was captured by the society?" she asked softly.

"When I was young, just starting school, my mother was invited to a social event at the house of another mother who had a child in my class. She was human and a friend. They'd known each other for the better part of that school year, and this meeting was to help organize an international day for my grade. Everything was fine until her husband came home and my mother saw his ring. He was a member of the Order. They'd only recently moved, and the home wasn't in our registers yet. She tried to leave, but he captured her.

"My father was a warrior, the Sagittarius member of the Zodiac Brotherhood. When he found out, he went berserk, but there was no way to get her out that wouldn't violate the peace accord. He negotiated. He traded himself for her."

"Oh my god, Mason..."

"By the terms of the accord, the Order is required to give captured dragons a choice. The first is bondage. For the rest of their existence, they're forced to serve a member of the Saint's Order. The Order has magic, Reagan. Different from ours but just as strong. They'll bind a captured dragon with a cuff that compels their obedience. For us, it's hell."

"What's the other choice?"

"To be hunted for sport to our death." I heard her gasp and wondered if I'd gone too far in telling her about this. Her fingers pressed into her lips, and tears formed in her eyes. "My father chose to be hunted and was murdered on Order grounds."

"Oh Mason..." Her throat bobbed on a swallow.

"So..." I took her hand in mine. "You going to this meeting could be a disaster for me... For us. I don't want you to give up your dream. Just maybe you could shift your focus to something else." I leaned in. "The good news is you have your own dragon to ensure you'll never be short of ideas."

She sighed. "Well then, I guess you and your dragon can relax, because I told my father I'd attend his awards banquet."

"Thank you." I pressed my lips to hers.

"Enough about me." She shifted on her stool. The place was still empty, and it was dark outside now. I hoped that meant we'd be alone until I could close the café.

"I don't think I could ever get enough about you."

"Likewise." She looked down into her cappuccino. "You made me a heart. No dragon today?"

"Just the one standing in front of you."

"You know this will keep me up all night." She lifted the cup.

"All part of my master plan."

She took a deep gulp.

"But I do have something to tell you," I said. "My uncle called today."

"Your uncle whom I assume is also a dragon."

"Yes. A dragon and a warrior for the brotherhood."

"A defender of the race, like your father?"

I nodded. "This is probably a lot for you to take in."

"I think I can keep up."

"Our Oracle has asked to speak with me. Connor thinks she's considering me for the brotherhood."

She set her cup down. "You'd become a warrior?"

"Maybe. Not immediately, but someday. It would be an honor if I was selected. It's in my blood. But being chosen is rare."

"Is it safe? After what you told me about your father..." Her body tensed with her worry for me, which both made me feel wanted by her and concerned that she might not be supportive of my new role. As my mate, she was the one person in the world who could keep me from taking the position if it was offered to me.

I squeezed her hand. "We're living under a peace accord, remember? Chances are I'll never see anything but a training field. Even if I do complete a mission for the Oracle, dragons are hard to kill. But this position is an important one, and it's one I've felt called to do for some time."

"When do you go to see this... Oracle?"

"Friday. I don't want you to worry about this, Reagan. It's a conversation, nothing more. I haven't even been offered the position yet. Besides, it gives me a chance to ask the Oracle about you."

"Me?"

"Human mates have to be approved by her before being recognized by our race. It's nothing to worry about.

She simply reads the stars and points out any possible future conflicts based on our charts."

She blew out a shocked breath. "I never thought my future with the man I love would be dictated by my horoscope."

I couldn't restrain my laugh. "Not exactly your horoscope." My brain slowly caught up with the rest of what she'd said. "You love me?"

She leaned her chin on her fist. "All the empirical evidence points to yes."

I glanced at the clock, then strolled around the counter and to the door, locking it and flipping the sign to CLOSED. Then I returned to where she was watching me from her stool, circled her waist with my hands, and hoisted her over my shoulder.

She squealed. "What are you doing?"

I smacked her on her ass. "Giving you some additional evidence."

Chapter Twenty-Three

REAGAN

I never thought of myself as the type of woman to be living out some kind of erotic dream, but there I was being carried on the shoulder of a man who definitely fit the bill. Swept off my chair and carried to the back room as if I weighed nothing, my body was ready for him, everything south of my midriff going haywire in anticipation of what was coming. Everything in me wanted to please him. I wasn't petite by any stretch of the imagination, but when he set me down on the desk, he did it with one arm. Shit, he was just so big, potent, virile. I wanted him like I'd never wanted anything or anyone.

Mason reached down for one of my feet, bracing it on his leg while he untied the laces of my boot and slipped it off. "If you don't want me to fuck you here in this room, you'll have to tell me to stop. My dragon will listen to you, but he's long past listening to me."

"Can't do that." I leaned in and brushed my lips across his. "If I don't have you inside me in the next five minutes, I think I'm going to combust."

I leaned back on my hands as he removed my other boot and then popped my hips up so he could strip off my jeans and thong. He planted a kiss on my hip, right where my torso met my leg, then skimmed his lips up my body until his stormy blue eyes were staring into mine.

"Combust if you want to. Dragons are fireproof."

Holy shit. My skin heated and I reached for his fly. Finding out that Mason was a dragon had been shocking, and I was still coming to terms with what it meant to be his mate. But one thing I didn't question was how much I desired him. I'd wanted him since the day we met, and right now I needed him with a physical intensity I hadn't known existed until now.

He reached behind his head and pulled his shirt off. I had his pants down and his dick in my mouth before it hit the floor. The growl of appreciation he gave me seemed to echo in the room and rumble in my bones. His fingers threaded into my hair, holding my head as he thrust to the back of my throat. I stared up at him, hollowed my cheeks, and sucked. He tasted like heaven. Smoke and spice and something uniquely him that made fire course through my veins.

"Need to be in you," he mumbled.

He pulled out of my mouth and lifted me until my legs wrapped around his hips and his erection was pressed between us. With supernatural grace and speed, he spun us around and flattened my back against the wall. Supporting me by the ass with one paddle-sized hand, he reached between us with the other and lined up the head of his cock with my opening.

I closed my eyes against the intense fullness as he pushed into me, stretching me to the limit. I panted for air, feeling like I was a balloon that had drifted too high in the stratosphere. My head was spinning. My heart thumped wildly in my chest. He was the best thing that could ever happen to me. He was like holding lightning between my thighs.

Mason's wings unfurled from his back, the muscles of his torso flexing with the effort. The dark, velvety wings seemed bigger in the small room. Maybe it was our position. Standing up like this, his huge body pressed into me, all I could see to either side of us was him. All I could smell was the smoky spice of dragon. All I could feel was him thrusting inside me again and again. It would have been overwhelming with anyone but him, but when his eyes met mine, their blue became my sky. His hold on me, grounded me, anchoring me to the Earth, to the moment.

God, he was deep and his thrusts hit me in just the right place.

"Do you know how good you feel, Reagan?" His breath skated across my cheek. "It's like you hold a missing piece of me and the only time I feel whole is when I'm inside you. I've waited my entire life for you."

The yearning in his voice, the gratitude for my being the thing he needed, pushed me over the edge. The physical pleasure was one thing, but my heart, my soul, seemed to stretch and unfold from the love pouring into me. My body clenched around him. I floated on a river of light, expanding, exploding, becoming. With a few more quick thrusts, Mason found his own release inside me. Afterward, he rested his forehead against the wall beside my head and slowly lowered my feet to the floor.

"Don't let me go," I said with a laugh. "I don't think I can stand yet."

He held me to him, his shoulder braced against the wall as if he was struggling to hold up his own weight. His heavily corded arms wrapped around me. With my ear pressed to his chest, my gaze sank to the floor where I noticed he was still wearing his pants and shoes.

"Mason?"

"Yeah."

"Can we go back to your place and do it in an actual bed?"

He kissed my temple, then pulled up his pants and tossed my clothes at me. "I'll drive."

Hours later, Mason and I had christened his shower, his sofa, and even the kitchen floor. We'd finished a night I'd forever remember as the sexual Olympics in his bed, where I was strewn across him, blissfully sore and with body parts that were about as useless as wet noodles.

"I think you broke me. I can't move," I said against his jaw.

He met my lips with a soft peck. "You'll be fine in the morning. Dragons have healing powers."

I scoffed. "I don't think I have enough dragon in me to enjoy that benefit."

He sighed, his eyes drifting closed. "If you want more dragon in you, you're going to have to wait. Even my kind needs to rest."

I snorted. "Good to know it's not just me. I feel like I've run a marathon." I repositioned myself in the crook of his arm.

"Seriously, you don't have to be a dragon to benefit from it. Humans who stay close to dragons experience enhanced creativity and intuition along with enhanced health. It's why the Order likes to keep us as prisoners. I think that's why my father chose the hunt. He knew as a mated warrior, his life would be too valuable to the Order had he chosen imprisonment."

I shivered. "The thought of them coming anywhere near you terrifies me."

"Likewise."

I was lying on his wing, but it didn't seem to bother him. I assumed it felt better to have them out than tucked away. We'd slept like that in the cave as well. I couldn't complain—the inside was soft as silk and cradled me perfectly. "Will it always be like this? It feels like I can't get enough of you."

"Some of what you're feeling is because I'm in my alignment. I was born under the Pisces sun sign, which means my drive to mate is at its highest now. Our alignment is the only time we can get our mates pregnant, so nature drives us to make every minute count."

I laughed. "Good thing I have an IUD. I don't think I'm ready for a dragon baby."

"Yet," he said with a little more gusto than I was strictly comfortable with. "When's your birthday?"

"December twenty-second. I'm a Capricorn."

"Then it will be this way again between the middle of December to the middle of January. And don't be surprised if you find yourself desperate to want that IUD out. You may not be a dragon, but nature has a funny way of reacting to a mating bond. During your alignment, babies may be all you can think about."

I chuckled at the thought. "Nature will just have to cool her jets on this one for a while. I plan to be married and settled before I have children."

"What do you consider settled?"

"Making enough money that I don't have to worry about how I'm going to feed them."

He grinned. "Got that covered."

"Hmm?"

"Dragons attract wealth. It just comes to us. You'll see the longer we're together. We are abundance magnets."

"What?" I rubbed my eyes.

"Don't think about it now."

Sleep tugged at me. "I should probably go home anyway."

"Stay," he said sleepily.

"Things are finally good with my dad. I don't want my staying out all night to become a bone of contention between us. When my mother died, a part of both of us died with her. Our family, our relationship, I feel like we've been going through the motions for years and finally, finally I'm connecting with him again."

He groaned. "The roads are icy. I'll drop you off."

"No. I left my car at the café. Drop me off there."

He shook his head, easing me off his wing. I watched in awe as he folded them away inside his body. They retracted through two six-inch crescent-shaped slits in his back that looked like silvery white scars. Definitely magic involved in that move. Even though he was a larger than-average man, those wings were far too big to fit inside Mason. "I'll drop you off, then drive to the café and return with your car."

"Then how will you get back?"

He slipped on his shirt, then leaned over and kissed me on my nose. "I'll fly."

I tucked my mussed hair behind my ears. "Can you do that? Won't people see you?"

He disappeared.

"Holy fuck!" I bounded to the other side of the bed. But then he moved, and I saw the

slightest distortion.

When he appeared again, he was in the doorframe. "Camouflage. It's enough, especially considering it's dark and rainy. Trust me, if anyone is out in this town tonight, I'll go right over their heads."

I blinked at him. "Is there anything else I should know about dragons?"

He stuck his foot in a shoe and tied the laces. "I can dreamwalk—get inside a human's head while they're sleeping. Sometimes when they're awake if they're daydreaming. I can change their dreams. Insert thoughts or ideas."

"Have you ever done that to me?" I asked nervously.

"No. And I never plan to, at least not without your permission."

Would there ever be a time I wanted my mate rattling around inside my head? I didn't think so. Some privacy was important.

I dressed quickly, feeling exhausted. Every time I thought I had my head around this thing that was happening between us, I learned something new and had to start processing it all over again.

"This is a lot, Mason. An entire species... an entire society... living among the one I was born into. It all seems surreal. I still have so many questions."

He wrapped an arm around my shoulders and led me toward the door, snatching my coat off the entryway hook and handing it to me on the way out. He didn't bother with a coat for himself, but it wasn't like he needed it. "Then I guess it's a good thing we have a lifetime to find the answers, together."

Ever the gentleman. A smoking-hot, fire-breathing, monster-becoming gentleman. I was the luckiest woman alive.

<h1 style="text-align:center">Chapter Twenty-Four</h1>

MASON

It was harder than I thought it would be to leave Reagan on Friday. We'd spent the past several nights either in bed or talking until the wee hours of the morning. She insisted on going home every night, even when I sensed she wanted to stay. I understood. She was rebuilding something with her father, something that had been broken since her mother died. I didn't want to ruin that for her.

Still, I couldn't wait to get the Oracle's blessing on our relationship. I planned to marry her the human way after making our mating official with my kind. Waking up every morning with her in my bed would be the answer to every prayer I'd ever said for myself—a blessing directly from the creator.

Visiting the Oracle had to come first though, and that

meant traveling to Cardinal Island. I dug the key out of my safe and hung it around my neck before exiting my apartment just as silver light broke the horizon. I flew straight up, until I was above the clouds, then right into the sun. Fisting the key, I uttered the spell that all dragons are given at their birth. "On wings and stardust, Creator carry me home."

The first rays of sunlight blinded me, and then I was landing on the shore of a great body of water next to a cobblestone-and-cedar lighthouse. My mother had taught me that the lighthouse was built thousands of years ago, in the beginning when it was just us and man, before the Order existed. This was a portal to our realm, Cardinal Island, a place where we planned and trained for what we needed to do in the human world. A place where the sky was always clear enough for the stars to shine bright enough to guide our direction.

An icy breeze came off the water, and I let myself inside the cozy lighthouse. A couple of recliners were positioned near a fireplace that was cold from disuse. Opposite the windows, a grandfather clock ticked, its pendulum swinging with the sound. The traditional clockface read 7:13 and the sun and moon dial showed the sun rising. There would be a full moon tonight. The second face, the spiral of gears that kept track of the celestial calendar, was made of a ring within a ring within a ring working together like cogs, showing the sun sign, the moon sign, and the ascending sign at every minute of every day. I stared at the two crescent shapes joined by a bar to look like the letter *H*, the sign for

Pisces. Seeing the symbol of my birth made me feel at home.

I slipped the key from around my neck. The gold head of it was etched with the same Pisces symbol, my birth sign. I slipped it into the keyhole of the glass case and turned the key two clicks. The scene outside the windows changed from light to dark to light again. In a way, it was unremarkable. Aside from the light, there was no sensation of movement. My stomach didn't drop. The ground didn't shift. It didn't feel like I'd gone anywhere.

But I had.

I removed my key, exited the lighthouse, and found myself in the town square of Cardinal Island. I had only seconds to appreciate the beauty of the village before a man the size of a small mountain plowed into my side and rubbed my head with his knuckles.

"Finally. I was worried you'd forgotten." Uncle Connor thumped my back and gave me one of his insolent grins. "Couldn't leave the bed of that mate of yours, I suppose."

I ran a hand through my hair, smoothing it down and punching him in the ribs, hard. He grunted and shoved me. Connor always reminded me of a Viking, tall and broad with dark blond hair and a beard that was trimmed short. His gray eyes were as steely as his personality, which was known to be unbendable at times, especially when he was working as a chef in his Manhattan restaurant.

"I'm right on time," I told him. "What are you doing here anyway? Don't you have a restaurant to run?"

He spread his hands. "Fuck if I was going to miss being here when the Oracle speaks directly to my only nephew, especially when she asked me to deliver the message!" He laughed in that way that came straight from his soul. We started walking toward the observatory. "I'll expect a full report once you're done. Meet me in the pub. Now go; she's waiting for you. Don't fuck it up."

I ENTERED THE OBSERVATORY THROUGH A SET OF OVERSIZED wooden doors that flew open at the slightest tug, proving far lighter than they should have been based on their size. The wood was like none I'd ever seen, smooth as oiled stone beneath my palm, but in its natural state with no paint or finish to enhance it. I wondered if whatever tree was used to make the entry even existed anymore.

"You must be Mason," a soft voice said. "I am Etheldred, an acolyte here at the observatory. I will take you to the Oracle." The acolyte spoke through a veil that completely obscured their face. "Please follow me."

Like all acolytes, Etheldred wore red silk robes that cloaked them from head to toe. From their veil to their foot wrappings, no skin showed. Mason had never known an acolyte personally, but all dragons understood that they were non-binary and celibate, their education and lives of service to the Oracle transcending gender and their biological drive to mate. Each of them studied at the side of the Oracle until midlife, prepared to replace her should the Oracle's time come to return to the creator. Their time here in this holy place was fully focused on helping her guide the dragon race. Acolytes could decide to return to society at any time to choose a mate or could choose to stay in the temple where they would eventually go up in flames and rejoin the universe. Generations of acolytes had come and gone over the course of this oracle's rule. Mason always thought it would be an especially hard life and often wondered what would drive someone like Etheldred to take up the role.

I followed the acolyte through a series of curved hallways connected by arched openings that stretched into darkness above. A labyrinth so complex that by the fourth turn, I felt like a rat searching for cheese. We finally arrived at what I assumed was the center of the observatory, and what I saw there almost knocked me on my ass. I gazed in wonder at the domed ceiling above me, instantly disoriented. It was morning outside, but in here, all I saw was a large expanse of night sky. The size and shape of the room gave me the sense of standing inside a telescope. All the constellations stretched out around me with impossible clarity.

"It's enchanted to always display the stars. The Oracle can see anytime, day or night," Etheldred explained. "Please wait here. Her holiness will join you in a moment." The acolyte bowed low and then left the way we'd come.

When I was finally able to pry my eyes away from the marvel above me, I discovered the rest of the room was just as strange and awe-inspiring. The space was filled with clocks. Wooden cuckoo clocks hung on the walls in a dozen shapes and sizes, grandfather clocks stood in the corners. Metal contraptions that made no sense to me spun and whirred on various surfaces around the room. There was even a digital clock in the shape of a small orange dog, it's eyes shifting left and right as the time ticked by in its chest.

Every clock told a different time.

I turned a tight circle, allowing the odd configuration to wash over me. It was marvelous, delightful, confusing. A neglected yard sale of timepieces. It was beyond my understanding.

"You wish to ask me about the girl."

I whirled to find an unremarkable older woman in a navy shirtdress standing behind me. Her wild, dark curls framed a clean face with wide eyes the color of espresso beans and a hooked nose. Crepey skin along her neck, exposed forearms, and the back of her hands, gave her the appearance of a human woman in her seventies, but I knew she was much older than that. One of the eyeteeth in her smile was slightly crooked. She looked old and plain, not at all what I was expecting.

"Oracle?"

She bobbed her chin. "You remind me of your father, Mason. Do you know you look like him?"

I swallowed. "So my mother says."

"She's right," she said with another bob of her chin.

She lowered her petite body onto a gold sofa with turned legs, flaring the cotton skirt of her dress over her knees and crossing her legs at the ankle. Her stature was surprisingly diminutive, although her power filled every molecule of space between us.

"You asked to see me?" I prompted.

"Let's discuss the girl first. Otherwise, you're liable to be thinking of her when we broach other matters."

"Uh, yeah, uh, Reagan. I'm in love with her and would like your permission to mate with her."

The Oracle smiled. "If we are to have a relationship, Mason Forge, son of Roger Forge, grandson of Wymond Forge, you must not lie to me. Know that I can see everything that ever was and could be. I know the truth as it has happened and a number of things that could be. You do not wish to ask my permission to mate her. You have already mated her. You are here to ask for my blessing so that your mating will be recognized by our kind."

I lowered my gaze, feeling ashamed. "Yes, Oracle. That is what I want."

"You may call me Sybil. Oracle is my title. Sybil is my name."

"Sybil," I repeated.

"I will consider your request while we discuss why I called you here."

I swallowed. The Oracle was said to be an ancient dragon, having lived with her mate for thousands of years. Being in her presence was like standing near an ocean whose waters were growing increasingly turbulent. One false move and a tidal wave would crush me.

"Why did you call me here?"

"Solomon has served me well as the Pisces warrior, but his future…" She tipped her head back and looked at the stars. "I am afraid that if he continues in his role, his life will be cut short in the coming years." Her voice took on a far-off, distracted quality. "His children will be important to the future of our race, but they only rise to their callings in timelines where he lives. I have asked him to step down."

A chill ran through me, ice forming in my veins. If Solomon continued in the brotherhood, she knew he would die. She could see his future. See it coming. She watched all the brothers. I couldn't stop myself from asking the question that immediately came to mind. "Did you know my father would die?"

Her gaze leveled on me, and her formerly warm features morphed into an expression more ancient and cunning. "I knew it. He knew it. Ultimately it was his choice, and he chose to trade himself for your mother. But what you really want to know is if I could have kept your mother from walking into the house where she was captured. The truth is, I wasn't watching for her future. I had no reason to. I didn't see it coming."

She hadn't known. I closed my eyes and let that truth sink in. I pictured what a life might have been like with my father if my mother hadn't fallen into the trap and the Order hadn't put him in the awful position that led to his death. The loss that weighed on my heart was heavy, but at least I knew the Oracle hadn't foreseen it. Hadn't been complicit in it.

"As I was saying, Solomon is stepping down and we have an opening in the brotherhood. I would like you to fill the position, Mason, but not because I value your life any less than his. The possible futures I see for you include far more scenarios with positive outcomes."

It was impossible to miss the nuance in her words. More but not all. I had a better chance of survival than Solomon, but not a certain chance. I thought about that, about what she was saying and what she wasn't. The Zodiac Brotherhood came with inherent risks. She was making me no promises.

"You understand, then, what I am asking of you."

I hadn't voiced my concerns, and she hadn't actually asked me anything, but when our eyes met, I saw it all there. She stood and paced the room, rubbing her palms together in tight circles, her eyes on the stars. "Other avenues exist aside from you. Those with less risk offer less reward for our kind. Dark times are coming, Mason. You feel the storm moving in already, don't you? Most of us do."

I *had* felt a change in the air. The gathering that Reagan had talked about was one sign that the society was active again. Assembling their forces. Readying themselves for something. It was just a feeling. A hunch. I wouldn't have gone so far as to say war was on the horizon. But then neither had she. *Dark times.* What did dark times mean but war? I frowned, my thoughts wandering to Reagan. If I did become a brother, I'd have access to training and magic that I could use to help protect her, but it all came with more risk to myself. I was okay with that.

"I'll do it," I said. "If you give Reagan and me your blessing."

Her eyes widened. "Don't you first want to know your own chances of survival?"

"I'd rather know Reagan's."

She nodded slowly. "You truly are a dragon mated. You'd die for her without a second thought."

"I would."

"Just like your father."

I bristled at that. "I don't think I'll ever be as brave as my father, but I'd like a chance to try. And I don't believe you would have asked me to do this if you didn't think I was the best thing for the race, not unless you already asked that person and they said no."

She smiled. "You were my first choice."

"I'm honored."

"Good. Then I suppose you'll want to know my decision about Reagan, although I have a feeling you'd move forward with your relationship with or without my blessing."

I said nothing. She was right and she knew it. I didn't have to tell her what she already knew.

Her lips tilted as if she held a delightful secret, and I braced myself. If she refused me, I wasn't sure what I'd do.

"You don't need my permission, Mason, or my blessing. Reagan is a dragon, a hybrid. Her mother was one of us."

My jaw dropped. I gaped at her like an adolescent, blinking, disbelieving. I'd suspected that Reagan had dragon blood. How else could she have found me at Smoke Hole? But a true hybrid? A mother who was a full-blooded dragon? "I don't understand. If that's true, why has she never shifted? Why can't she use her wings?"

Sybil gripped her jaw and gazed up at the stars again. "I see darkness around your mate. Normally a dragon's past is clear to me and it is the future that is hazy with possibilities, but Reagan's past is as opaque as her future. Something about her current circumstances has kept her inner dragon from emerging. Perhaps her mother's death is to blame. Living solely among humans has dulled her shifter instincts. It's possible that she might shift once she's lived with you for a time."

The repercussions of what Sybil was saying to me sank in slowly. "Then Reagan is my true mate. I can register us in the book. I can marry her."

The Oracle nodded, still studying the stars, but then her face took on a worried expression. "You must teach her, Mason. The darkness I see surrounding her, it's choking her. Take her from that place she lives. As soon as possible."

I didn't like the sound of that and wondered if what she was seeing had anything to do with Reagan's father. Reagan had felt the need to move out. What she'd told me suggested the man might be stifling her. I wondered if there was more to it.

"I'll leave at sunrise."

She turned toward me once more and placed her

hands over her heart. "Then welcome, warrior, to the Zodiac Brotherhood. I will send word with your uncle when your ascension is imminent."

With a shallow bow, she left me, and Etheldred escorted me out into the sunlit village of Cardinal Island, my mind racing with possibilities.

Chapter Twenty-Five

REAGAN

"Dad?" I walked into his office, completely confused. "Our driver just told me to be ready by five thirty. I thought your event was at seven?"

He gave me a glance while continuing to type something on his computer. "It is, but the event is in Harpers Ferry."

I froze. "Harpers Ferry?"

"Yes. That's where the ceremony is taking place."

I bristled. It couldn't be, could it? "What organization is honoring you?"

Dad stopped typing. "They call themselves the Saint's Order. They're similar to the Freemasons. It's a networking organization."

My face grew cold, and I knew all the color had drained from my complexion.

"You okay, Peanut?" He shot me a concerned look.

"Fine." My mind spun its tires, but my thoughts were like my Jetta caught in the mud—going nowhere. I couldn't think of a single excuse to not attend that night.

"Good. I'm so glad you're coming. This past week, forming a relationship with you again, it's meant a lot to me. I'm not a man who usually says what he's feeling, but I want you to know that."

Shit. The genuine warmth Dad was projecting was something I hadn't seen in a really long time, and my heart swelled. I had to be careful how I handled this. What we'd built the past few days was still fragile. I told him I felt the same way and then retreated to my room to brainstorm what to do.

I couldn't go, obviously. I'd promised Mason I wouldn't. But then, as I thought about it more, when I'd made that promise, it was based on keeping him safe. His dragon was incapable of staying away from me as my mate. But that fear was moot. Mason would be gone until tomorrow. Even if I wanted to talk to him about this, I couldn't. He'd told me the place he was going, Cardinal Island, was completely disconnected from the rest of the world. Which meant he wasn't at risk because I'd be in and out before he returned. I believed the Saint's Order was a threat to dragons, but I was human and would be with my father the entire time. They weren't a risk to me.

Flopping onto my back on my bed, I stared at the ceiling. Litz jumped up next to me and snuggled in. I could feign illness, but I was a terrible liar, and if I poisoned my relationship with my dad, I knew I'd regret it.

I draped an arm over my eyes. What would happen if I did go? I'd be safe with my dad and I could gather information on the Order for Mason, even if I didn't report on it. A dragon couldn't do that, and there would never be another opportunity for me to have insider access. Going, and recording everything I saw, might actually be the best thing I could do for Mason and the rest of the dragons.

I told myself that he'd forgive me for this. I believed, if we'd been able to discuss it by phone, he might even encourage me under the circumstances. Sitting up, I reached for my phone.

"Hey, Imani... I need your help."

LATER THAT EVENING, DAD'S DRIVER PULLED UP IN FRONT OF AN enormous Craftsman-style house that reminded me of a Frank Lloyd Wright on steroids. I would have never found this place on my own. It wasn't so much in Harpers Ferry as in the area on the edge of town, nestled within acres and acres of private wooded land. It might be a Harpers Ferry address, but this place was off the map.

Casually, I used my phone to drop a pin for Imani. I was wired with a tiny camera that was hidden in a rosette on the strap of my dress. Everything I saw tonight was being transmitted to her equipment and recorded. She was also my back up in case anything went wrong. I understood these people were dangerous. It was important to have a backup plan. But with the layout of this place and the security, she'd be lucky to get her van within a mile of the house. I was hoping that didn't affect the transmission.

"You might as well leave your phone in the car." My dad cast a sideways glance at the device in my hands and winked. "They'll confiscate it at the door if you try to bring it inside."

I handed it to the driver. "Mind watching this for me, Mr. Daniels?"

"Pleased to help, Ms. Bailey." The elderly man tapped the edge of his cap.

"Shall we?" Dad opened the door and stepped out, extending his hand toward me.

I slid across the seat and took his fingers in mine. I appreciated the help considering the full skirt I was wearing made everything more difficult.

Once I was out of the car, I noticed we weren't the only ones arriving. Dozens of older men and women were making their way toward the door from cars even fancier than ours. The men wore expensive suits, and the women dripped with jewels. No one in the Saint's Order was hurting for money. I'd learned as much from my research. But I hadn't known so many women were involved in the Order. Every ring-wearer we'd come across had been a man, and I'd assumed it was a fraternal organization. I made a note to myself to check if any women also wore the signet rings.

We reached the door where a balding man in a suit and earpiece patted me and my father down. I casually placed my hands on my collarbones as if trying to keep them out of the way when I was really covering the flower and its hidden camera. He searched my bag too before gesturing for us to enter.

Inside, I followed a red velvet runner between tall arrangements of fresh flowers to a massive ballroom. A jazz band played on a dais in the far corner. People danced and mingled. A waiter with a tray of champagne coasted by us almost immediately, and Dad grabbed a glass. He offered me one too, but I refused. I wanted to be sober and attentive. The best thing I could do for Mason was to be strategic about my conversations.

Everything I recorded could be used later.

"Richard, I'm so glad you've chosen to join us tonight." A tall, white-haired man emerged from the crowd, extending his hand toward my father.

Beside him, another man, about my father's age, greeted us with a shallow smile. Several things struck me at once about the couple. Although the white-haired man looked to be about eighty, he was straight-backed and moved with the grace of someone half his age. The man at his side was even fitter, carrying himself with the sort of long and lean composure of a professional athlete. His brown hair was peppered with gray over the ears, and his eyes were the color of gunmetal. When he looked at me, he seemed to see straight into my soul. By the way the backs of their hands brushed, I assumed the two men were a couple. They moved almost in lockstep with each other, as if they'd been together a long time.

My father clasped the older man's hand in his own and shook. "Stefan, allow me to introduce you to my guest for the evening. This is my daughter, Reagan. Reagan, this is Stefan Cifarelli and..." His gaze drifted to the other man.

"Donovan," the man beside Stefan said, by way of introduction. He shook my father's hand, then reached for mine as a chill traveled through me and the smoky scent of singed rose petals met my nose.

I shook Donovan's hand and knew instantly that he was a dragon. And not just any dragon. Mason had told me that Donovan had sacrificed himself for the peace treaty between dragons and the Order. But this Donovan didn't look like a prisoner. He looked like Stefan's date.

"Nice to meet you both," I muttered, trying to work it out in my head.

My hand had just slipped from Donovan's when a third man, one with dark brown waves and eyes the color of coffee grounds, arrived.

"Is this our new recruit?" the newcomer said, gesturing toward my father.

Recruit? I'd thought my father was being *honored* by the Saint's Order. He couldn't be... joining.

"Yes, meet Richard Bailey and his daughter Reagan. This is my son, Roman." Stefan gestured toward the younger man, and my father immediately took his hand in a firm grip. But then Roman's gaze fell on me, and I watched something like disgust pass through his expression. It was gone as fast as it came, but he did not offer me his hand. My intuition sent up a geyser of red flags. Roman had issues, and he didn't like women much.

"Richard, looking forward to welcoming you into the fold," Roman said, placing his left hand on top of their coupled rights. "We'll start the ceremony at the top of the hour. See you then."

Roman dipped his chin and then turned to his father. "May I speak with you alone for a moment?" Stefan excused himself to follow his son toward the nearest door, leaving Donovan behind with us.

I leaned toward my dad and whispered, "Are you joining the Order tonight? I thought you said you were being honored."

He nodded. "Honored with an invitation to join."

I opened my mouth to garner more of an explanation, but Donovan interrupted. "You'll have to excuse Roman's abrupt departure. When it comes to the Order, he's all business."

Dad sipped his champagne, standing up straighter and shifting away from me. "Successful men don't linger over trivialities," he said lightly.

I scowled, realizing that in this instance, we were the triviality.

Donovan darted a glance at me again. "Richard, I wonder if you'd allow me to dance with Reagan? I'm sure you want to mingle with some of the other initiates and Order members." He gestured toward the crowd.

"Yes, yes. If you're comfortable with that, Reagan?" Dad was already eying the crowd.

"I'd love to." I slipped my hand into Donovan's and allowed him to lead me onto the dance floor.

Donovan was a practiced dancer, and he expertly spun us across the floor. Once we were in step but far enough away from the other dancers, he lowered his mouth to my ear and whispered, "What the hell are you doing here?"

I wasn't sure what he meant. I'd just met him. "I'm here to support my father. He's becoming a member," I said matter-of-factly.

His eyes narrowed. "I know what you are. And I suspect Roman does too, which is why he's speaking to his father right now."

I swallowed, feeling uneasy. "I don't know what you're talking about."

He scoffed, those steely eyes meeting mine. "I have to hand it to you. You've masked your scent well, but it won't help you here. Once the ceremony starts, the magic forces our true nature to the surface. Trust me on this, child. Get out while you still can. Whatever you came to do, you'll fail, and I won't be able to help you."

I raised my brows, suddenly confused. "Oh, I'm not..." I gave a low laugh. "I'm not like you."

He closed his eyes for a beat. "Then, you know what I am."

Was there any risk of admitting it? My gut told me I could trust Donovan, but why take the risk? My lashes fluttered and I tried my best to keep my cool, but inside my heart was thundering and I knew the palm that was nestled in his had begun to sweat.

He brought his nose close to my skin and inhaled deeply. "Forge? That would mean the son?"

I gaped at him.

Understanding sparked in his eyes. When he spoke again, his voice was so low I could hardly hear him. "You're *his*."

That was a bit of information I hadn't meant to share, so I glanced away as he danced us toward the other end of the floor.

A muscle in his jaw popped. "Reagan, where's your mother tonight? I'd think she'd want to be here for your father."

I swallowed. "My mom died when I was young."

He shook his head, his face paling. He leaned in so that his lips were to my ear. "You've made a mistake. If you love Mason, you need to find a way out of this house as soon as possible. Walk out the door and run. Don't look back."

By the time he pulled away, the song had come to an end. We stopped and separated, Donovan's face forming a wooden smile as his hands came together to clap for the jazz band. I joined in, my chest still rising and falling too fast as I digested our interaction. The room was hot. I couldn't catch my breath.

The singer brought the microphone to his lips. "I'm told the ceremony is about to begin. Initiates, please descend to the ritual room using the staircase on the left.

Guests, please use the door to the right for the observation area."

Donovan glanced back at me, bowed his head, and moved to join Stefan, who had reentered the room and was waiting for him near the stairs. I didn't see Roman.

"Reagan, there you are." Dad hugged my shoulders excitedly. "Wish me luck, darling. I'll see you after the ceremony."

"Good luck, Dad." I kissed his cheek, smiling brightly. He took off like an excited child in the direction of the stairs on the left.

"This way, ma'am," a servant said, pointing toward a door on the right. A line had formed as the group, mostly women, made their way toward the observation room. I glanced back at the initiates. All men. So I'd been right about that at least.

I looked directly at the man ushering me toward the door and said, "Can you direct me to the ladies' room please?"

He pointed toward a separate exit and mumbled, "To the left."

I took off at a fast clip, finding the bathroom right where he'd indicated. I locked the door behind me and leaned my hands on the counter, staring at myself in the mirror. Donovan must have been able to smell Mason on me. That's why he'd originally assumed I was a dragon like him. That shouldn't have surprised me—we'd pretty much spent the past three days in bed together and, although I'd showered, I had to think that a dragon's sense of smell was better than any human's. If Donovan knew and he belonged to these people, he might tell. Was I putting Mason in danger by being here?

I sighed. I was so close. If I walked out that door right now and went to the observation room, I'd have the story. No one had ever published an exposé on the Saint's Order. I'd have video and a first-person account of not only a gathering of the secret society but an induction ceremony, all from the inside. I'd already seen faces of politicians I recognized and wealthy business owners. I could report that too. I didn't have to mention anything about dragons.

But if Donovan knew who I was and who I was mated to, doing what I came to do could hurt Mason. I wasn't willing to do that. With a deep sigh, I moved for the door, then cursed when I realized I didn't have my phone. I could leave, but how would I call for a ride? How would I tell my father I left without him? After a second of thinking through scenarios, I turned the flower on my strap to face me and whispered, "Abort mission. Meet me at my pin. I'm coming out."

Imani wouldn't let me down. She was watching all of this. I needed to get out of here.

Resolved to leave, I unlocked the door and stepped out into the hall. And ran smack into Roman Cifarelli.

Chapter Twenty-Six

REAGAN

"Excuse me," I said, trying to push around Roman to get to the door. "I need to get something from my car."

He flashed his teeth in an expression I couldn't call a smile. "I'm afraid that's impossible. For security reasons, all cars were asked to leave the property and return at midnight."

"Oh." I needed to get away from this guy. I was getting a major creeper vibe. I turned and pointed in the direction I'd come. "I'll just show myself to the observation room then."

He tipped his head, his smile widening. I could tell he was trying to be charming, but my gut told me to run, run, run. "They've already closed and locked the doors, but no matter, you're in luck. I have a private observation area downstairs. I'll make sure you're comfortable."

"That's not necessary—"

He grabbed my wrist in an iron grip and dragged me down the hall.

"Roman, you're hurting me," I said loudly.

One of the servants heard and glanced in my direction but went about whatever they were doing.

"I'm sick," I said, grasping at straws even as I tripped after him. "That's why I was in the bathroom. I need... stomach medicine from my driver. If you could just call him back."

He opened a door and forced me through it and then down a flight of stairs. I was openly struggling now, kicking and scratching, trying my best to free myself, but his grip on my shoulders was as intractable as iron, and although I was protesting loudly, there was no one to hear me.

Roman opened another door and thrust me inside a dark room. I stumbled, falling to the carpeted floor with a grunt. By the time I fought around my full skirt to scramble back to my feet, he'd closed the door, cutting off the only source of light. The click of a lock engaging sent my heart racing.

"Hey!" I screamed. I ran to the door, tried the knob and found it locked. I banged on it with my fists. "What the hell? Let me out."

I heard footsteps behind me, and then a hand landed on my shoulder. "I told you to run." Donovan's voice, and it sounded forlorn.

"Donovan? Where are we? Why are the lights off?" I

patted the wall beside the door, feeling for the light switch.

"You don't need the lights, Reagan. Let your eyes adjust," he said calmly but with a note of frustration.

I whirled toward his voice. "I can't see in the dark," I snapped. But as I looked in his direction, the outline of his body came into view. I blinked and blinked again, and I could see him. Not like I could in full light but clearly enough to make out his sad smile.

"I tried to warn you," he said softly.

"I tried to leave," I admitted. "Roman caught me and brought me here. Why am I here? Do they know about Mason? Are they using me—?"

He snorted. "Reagan, I wish I wasn't the one to have to tell you this, but your being here has nothing to do with him. You're here because of what you are, not because of what he is."

My head felt like someone had replaced my brain with cotton balls. "Huh? What, because of my father or something?"

"I suspect your father had something to do with it. He must have known."

"Known what?"

"Tell me about your mother, Reagan."

My eyes burned. "What has she got to do with anything?"

"Because she's half of who you are."

"Her name was Teryn, and she was beautiful. The best mom ever. She didn't work outside the home, but she volunteered all the time. She died when I was eleven of a heart defect."

"Did you see her body after she died?"

"What kind of a question is that?" I didn't like how he was drilling me. I should be the one demanding answers. Why was I a prisoner here?

"Please," Donovan said. "I just need to be sure."

"No. My father said I was too young and he didn't want me to remember her like that. She was cremated."

Donovan shook his head. "She was a dragon, Reagan."

Everything stopped, and I simply gaped at him. The idea was ridiculous. Then I remembered that Mason had said he thought I had dragon's blood. "Maybe she was descended from a dragon, but she couldn't be a dragon." She couldn't, could she?

"You are a dragon, Reagan. I can smell you and so can Roman. His hunting skills are unparalleled. That's why you're here with me."

"What?" My voice was breathy, disbelieving.

"I'm not sure how it happened with your father and your mother. Maybe they were in love. Maybe he had something on her. But he must have known."

"Why are you saying this?" I said, warm, wet tears sliding down my face.

"Because any minute now, that curtain is going to open and we are going to be part of the ritual of initiation. The Saint's Order will perform a spell that will force us to shift into our dragon forms. For me, it will be easy. For you, being a hybrid and having never shifted before...

I won't lie to you Reagan—it will be painful. Once we've shifted, they will drain our power and use it to fuel dark magic."

I shook my head. Me? A dragon? He might as well have told me I had three legs. "I'm not a dragon, Donovan." I spread my hands. "Look at me. I'm human. Nothing more."

We both whirled as a floor-to-ceiling curtain opened, letting in light from a scene out of some late-night horror movie. Donovan and I were in a large empty room behind a wall of glass. On the other side was a cave filled with white candles. At least twenty men, dressed in hooded white robes with red crosses on the front, circled an archaic symbol with a cauldron at its center. The cauldron was slightly misshapen, as if it were fashioned by hand a long time ago. It struck me as positively primeval, big enough for two men to fit inside. Its belly glowed with an eerie electric-blue light, and fog mounded over its edges.

I chuckled a little under my breath. "Whoever was responsible for the aesthetics really leaned into the secret society vibe. Is that a string of blue lights and some dry ice in the cauldron?"

Donovan didn't answer. I glanced in his direction to see him staring at the palm of his hand. A series of scars ran the length of it and up his arm as well, healed but raised and white.

"No." He gave a low, sad laugh. "No dry ice. Just my blood."

"Your blood glows in the dark?"

"It does when it's used to power an ancient spell." He gave a heavy sigh. "At least it comes from me now and not dragons they've slain."

My mind scrambled to remember what Mason had told me about this dragon and to piece it together with what was right in front of me. If I'd understood correctly, Donovan had been a warrior for the dragon race. He'd sacrificed himself in exchange for the peace treaty. The Order agreed to no longer hunt dragons outside its domain. In return, they got Donovan. Mason said that just being near a dragon made a person more innovative and enhanced their health. But there was more. His blood could be used for magic.

I stepped closer to the glass, narrowing my eyes to see what was in the cauldron. It was filled with rounded steel... handles? Oh my god... *Swords*. I made out the flat edge of a blade.

What the actual hell?

I spun to face Donovan again. "Jesus Christ, are they using your blood to make the magical weapons that can kill your kind?"

Donovan nodded once, despondent. "They can't use the weapons unless a dragon comes onto their property willingly."

I raised a hand to my heart. "You mean me!"

He tipped his head. "Yes. You shouldn't have come here, Reagan."

"I didn't know. I didn't know any of this." He had to be wrong about my mother. It was impossible.

"My relationship with Stefan is complicated. After all

these years, he... Sometimes I can sway him. I'll try to talk him into releasing you."

I couldn't even think about that. I was still reeling over there being any chance I was an actual dragon. Surely they wouldn't kill me if I didn't sprout wings like they expected me to.

"We come together tonight to perform the ceremony to bind our new members to our cause." Stefan raised his hands and began to speak, calling our attention back to the ceremony. "In the beginning, Saint George saw the danger of dragons, how they whispered to women and the poor. Gave them sinful ideas about rising up and challenging their God-ordained place in the world. Knowing that the dragon's presence was causing chaos among the people of his village, George slew the dragon with a sword blessed with magic given to him by a dark, avenging angel. Afterward, George established the Saint's Order, transcribing the angel's instructions on how to hunt, trap, and kill dragons. Now, thousands of years later, we carry on this tradition. Although the days of slaying dragons are mostly behind us, we continue George's work, maintaining the values that existed in his time through a network of influential leaders."

The men rumbled, "Let it be so."

"Initiates, please step forward and remove your hoods." Three men stepped closer to the cauldron and revealed their faces. My father was beaming as if he was having the night of his life. Did he even know I was trapped in here? I banged on the glass. "Dad? Dad!"

"It's soundproof," Donovan said softly. "Even if it wasn't, he won't help you. Trust me on this."

"Of course he'll help me. He's my father," I protested. "He's not going to leave me in here." I waved my arms, trying to get my father's attention, but his back was to me.

"Drake Johnson, what do you offer in exchange for us accepting you as one of our own?" Stefan asked.

The dark-haired man on the end of the row of initiates withdrew a rolled paper from inside his robes. "The deed to my Montana farm." He handed the paper to Roman, who handed it off to a hooded figure behind him.

"Your offering is acceptable," Roman stated.

"James Oakland, what do you offer in exchange for us accepting you as one of our own?"

The bald man next to my father handed what looked like a contract to Roman. "I offer my legal services free of charge to the Order for the next five years."

Roman examined the paperwork, then passed it back to the hooded figure. "Your offering is acceptable."

"Richard Bailey, what do you offer the Order in exchange for us accepting you as one of our own?"

"I offer my daughter, who is half-dragon."

A high-pitched sound exited my mouth, and it felt as if he'd punched me hard in the stomach, knocking the breath from my lungs. This couldn't be happening. This couldn't be real.

"I'm so sorry, Reagan," Donovan said, new moisture in his eyes glinting in the blue light.

He'd tried to warn me. He'd tried to help me.

The men turned around to face the window and us behind it. The light came on in our room, blinding me. I rubbed my eyes and found them wet with my tears. Once they adjusted, I met my father's gaze. I'm not sure what I expected, but his expression was colder, more heartless, than I could ever imagine.

"In order to prove the worthiness of your gift, we must see her shift," Roman said, "but as you've shared with us that she's never done so, we will draw the beast out with magic."

I stiffened as Roman walked to the cauldron and started chanting in, what I could only assume, was Latin before scraping an offering of fruit and herbs into the pot.

Pain rolled through me like I'd been stabbed in the back of the shoulders and both hips. I grabbed my sides and screamed.

"Don't fight it," Donovan said. "Open the door and let her out."

Open the door? What the hell was he talking about? It felt like all my cells were on fire. There was no door to open. I was being ripped apart, every joint screaming in agony.

"Help me," I begged Donovan.

In answer, he stripped out of his shirt. A thick metal cuff decorated his left wrist and glowed a reflective blue as he moved. The rest of his clothing hit the floor, and a second later, his arms stretched to the ground. As I watched, his legs buckled, bent backward toward his elongating spine. It took less than thirty seconds for him to transform into a dragon the color of stainless steel. The same color as his eyes.

I had only a second to appreciate the size and beauty of the beast before me when another blast of excruciating pain rolled through me. I pitched forward, catching myself on my knees. My back burned as if someone had speared through my scapula with two meat hooks. I cried out, trying to reach the spots with my fingers.

A sharp crack met my ears, followed by a slice as if my skin was splitting. I screamed again, and this time something changed. The weight on my back seemed to spread and shift. It was like being crammed inside a too-tight sleeping bag and suddenly getting free and spreading my arms. I breathed, rolling with the relief, and saw a bright pink wing swipe just outside the corner of my eye. With equal parts wonder and horror, I took in the fuchsia paws that were once my hands, the torn dress that no longer fit my body, and the barbed tail that wrapped around my feet.

I glared at my father and at the other men who watched me. Glared through my reflection without initially realizing it was mine. A pink dragon stared back at me from the glass. A dragon like Mason and Donovan, although significantly smaller. Next to the mammoth silver dragon beside her, she looked like an adolescent. But she had horns, teeth, and claws. I looked around the room for this dragon and found it was only me and

Donovan in the room. I looked back at the glass. Back at Donovan. It was me. I was this dragon.

Staring straight at my father, pure fiery rage filling every corner of my being, I roared my hatred and grief as loud and as long as I could.

Roman laughed, his eyes as dark as coal. "Your offering is acceptable."

Chapter Twenty-Seven

MASON

Connor kept me up late, singing songs at the Compass Point, the pub on Cardinal Island that overlooked the sea and sported a nautical navigation vibe. The Viking insisted we celebrate my mating and my future as a warrior, each celebration entailing enough alcohol to pickle a full-sized dragon. Thank the creator that dragons recovered quickly, because after what the Oracle had told me about Reagan, I couldn't waste the morning on a hangover.

I planned to ask her to marry me and to move into my place as soon as possible if she'd agree to it. The Oracle's visions were woolly, but whatever darkness was wrapped around Reagan, I vowed to eliminate it. If I had anything to do with it, her days would be filled with love and light from here on out. Once she was in my home and in my bed, we could slowly address the possibility that she might shift, that she was as much dragon as human. It was big news, and I couldn't wait to share it with her.

I was up, through the lighthouse, and back at my apartment the second the first rays of sunlight hit the horizon. I called Reagan immediately to tell her the news, knowing I'd probably be waking her but unable to wait. The call went straight to voicemail. I flew to her house and up to her window. When she wasn't there, I tucked my wings away and knocked on the front door.

A Hispanic woman in a uniform opened it. "Can I help you?"

"I'm here to see Reagan," I said softly, aware that it was early, just after sunrise.

"Ms. Bailey isn't here. Can I give her a message on your behalf?"

I tried to look as confused as possible, which wasn't hard. I didn't have to fake it. "Do you know where she is? We had a date for coffee this morning."

The woman frowned. "Ms. Bailey is still in Harpers Ferry with her father. They'd planned to return last night, but he called to let us know they decided to stay another day to enjoy the sights. I'm sure she'll call to explain as soon as she's up."

An ice grenade exploded in my chest, sending shards to every corner of my body. Her father's event was in Harpers Ferry. The gathering of the Saint's Order was in Harpers Ferry. It was too much of a coincidence to draw any conclusion other than that they attended the meeting together. But was her father already a member or becoming one? Had her father tricked her into attending or was she still investigating the Saint's Order for her story? And if they were still there, what did that mean for Reagan?

I thanked the woman, then took off for my car at a run. I'd just slid behind the wheel when my phone rang. It was my uncle. *No, no, no, no, no.* "Connor?"

"Donovan was able to get a message through." Connor's tone was sullen. "They have Reagan, Mason. He couldn't give me details. You know he was risking everything—"

"Where is she?" I gritted out, starting the engine.

"Meet me in Harpers Ferry. I'll give you the address then. We go in together or not at all."

"You expect me to delay going in when they have my mate?" My hands shook so hard I almost dropped the phone.

"No. Which is why I'm not giving you a choice." The line went dead.

The bastard hung up on me without giving me the addy. I tore out of the Baileys' driveway like it was on fire and reached Harpers Ferry in record time. Connor was waiting for me and dropped me a pin to his location, a back road in the middle of nowhere. I was surprised to see who was with him.

"Hey Mason," Imani said. Unlike when I'd met her in the café, she didn't look polished. Instead, she looked like she hadn't slept in two days. It worried me how wrecked she looked, given the circumstances.

"What are you doing here? Where's Reagan?"

She tipped her head in the direction of a white utility van behind them. "Come on in and I'll show you. I couldn't explain it if I tried. There's some freaky-ass shit going on inside this house, and Connor here convinced me you're the ones who can help."

Connor flashed in insouciant grin. "We had a little chat. She is most definitely on our side here. You need to see the video, Mason. Reagan was wired."

My heart sank. If Reagan was wired, that meant she knew what she was doing going in there. She'd intended to investigate and report on the Saint's Order, despite my warning her against it and her promise to stay away. I closed my eyes and cursed as her betrayal opened a wound in my chest that hurt like she'd blown a hole through me. If I'd been a human man, it might have been enough for me to leave her to her fate.

This was no simple broken promise. She'd tarried with the people who killed my father. She knew the risk to me and to my kind and had done it anyway. As worried as I was for her, I was angry too, so angry that I'd be afraid what I'd do if she were standing in front of me. But my anger wouldn't get her out of there. She was my mate, and while I might punish her for what she'd done once I had her in my arms again, I would not leave what was mine in the hands of the enemy.

"Mason?" Connor barked.

"Yeah?"

"You okay, buddy?"

"No. But I will be. Show me the video."

Imani led us into the back of the van and handed me

a pair of headphones; then she cued up the recording. I watched as Reagan entered the house. Jesus, the place was enormous. Order members spared no expense. I sat up straighter when I saw Donovan and heard him warn her to run. When she left the queue to go to the bathroom and told Imani to meet her because she was coming out, my stomach clenched. She'd changed her mind. She'd tried to leave.

"I came immediately," Imani said. "But she never made it out of the house."

"Roman," I hissed. The sight of him manhandling her into the stairwell made my blood boil and my skin itch to shift.

"Easy, Mason." Connor placed a hand on my shoulder. "We'll get her back. We will."

"Keep watching." Imani raised an eyebrow and pointed at the screen.

For a few minutes, I simply took in what was happening. This was the first time I'd ever seen the inner workings of an Order event. None of us, aside from Donovan, had ever been inside and come out alive, and Donovan had to be careful how much and how often he communicated with us. But here it was, an actual Order initiation.

"Fuck. Fuck. That fucking bastard." I got to my feet when I heard her father openly trade her for his membership, handing her over like she was a stack of bills. Like she wasn't even a person. And then my stomach turned as I watched them force her to shift.

I had to remove the headphones. I couldn't listen to

her scream. Not anymore. My jaw locked and my eyes burned as I watched her slow and painful metamorphosis in the reflection of the glass, and then her dress must have ripped off because the camera stopped working.

"She hid the camera in a flower on her strap, and it transmitted wirelessly to me. It must have landed face down when it fell off her because those were the last images I received. But it wasn't the end of the recording. If you put your headphones back on, you can hear what happens next." Imani nudged the headphones back toward my head and I put them on, listening although the screen had gone black.

Initiates, extend your hands over the cauldron. Choose a sword. Draw it out and hold it above your head. Murmurs of amazement. *Wear these rings, always, for only with them do you carry the magic to kill our enemies.* Applause. More murmurs. Whimpering.

Fuck, that was Reagan crying. Had she shifted back?

They're going to give you a choice. That was Donovan's whisper, close to the recording device. *They'll offer you the option to be a member's prisoner or to be hunted for sport on these grounds. Your father will want you to take the first option. You'll be auctioned off. No doubt he plans to buy you. Listen to me, Reagan. Don't fall asleep. Not yet. I know you're tired and I know it hurts, but this is important. Choose the hunt. The hunt is the only way they'll let you outside without a cuff like mine. Once the cuff is on, there's no chance of rescue, do you understand? Choose the hunt. If you can make it to the oak tree at the center of the property, you'll have a chance. The brotherhood can't interfere anywhere else on the property. It has to be there.*

Another whimper.

Repeat what I said, Reagan. Now, before they come for us.

Choose... hunt... God, it sounded like she was barely conscious. *Oak tree.*

Good girl. Now sleep. You'll need it.

I tore the headphones off and tossed them on the counter. "Fucking hell, why would he tell her to choose the hunt? Dozens of Order members against a newly shifted dragon without any weapons. If she tries to shift, it will take too long and they'll kill her. If she doesn't shift, she has no way to defend herself or wings to even attempt an escape. She's as good as dead if she chooses the hunt. What the hell was Donovan thinking!" It was like suffering my father's death all over again. I couldn't do it. I couldn't watch them kill her this way. I roared until Imani had to cover her ears.

Imani lowered her hands as soon as I petered out. "You finished with your little tantrum, dragon man? You ready to talk solutions now?"

Connor chuckled and thrust an oversized elbow into my shoulder. "I like her. I think we should keep her."

Leaning back in her chair, the stare she gave Connor threatened to melt his face off. "I am going to let that one pass because I want to get my friend back and you two are my best bet of making that happen. But know this, Connor, no one *keeps* Imani Harris. Ever. Fuck around and find out."

The Viking cleared his throat. "Sorry. No one will be keeping anyone."

"Now that we have that straight, I think I can explain why Donovan told her to go for the oak tree. After I saw this last night, I used a drone to explore the back forty on this place. I found the oak tree in question, and something else just as interesting."

She brought up another video, and I leaned in. The drone zoomed through the trees until it reached a massive white oak tree with a trunk at least four feet in diameter. The drone lowered, focusing its tiny light on a plaque in front.

"Holy shit," Connor murmured. "Imani, you are amazeballs, woman!" He reached out his fist, and she bumped it reluctantly with hers.

I read what the plaque said out loud. "Landmark tree, property of Harpers Ferry municipal government, in commemoration of the meeting place of abolitionist John Brown in the slave revolt of 1859."

Imani held up two fingers. "You may not be able to set foot on these bastards' private property, but that tree isn't on their property. That belongs to the city. And although it's surrounded by their property and therefore inaccessible on foot, my drone was able to reach it just fine."

"Which means we can fly in," I said, folding my arms.

"Let freedom ring, motherfuckers." Her red lips stretched into a grin. "So, you guys can do it, right? You got those dragony powers." She pointed vaguely in my direction. "And he's all..." She quirked a lip and waved at the general mounds of muscle stretching Connor's shirt.

"We can and we will," I said.

Connor stroked the short scruff on his chin. "They'll wait until nightfall. Too risky in full light."

"So, we bide our time and hope to hell that she takes Donovan's advice." I ran my hand down my face and tried not to think about the distance between the house and the oak tree.

"And if she doesn't?" Imani darted a glance between Connor and me.

I looked her straight in the eye and told her the truth. "Then I offer myself in exchange for her freedom."

Chapter Twenty-Eight

REAGAN

I woke up in a cell, wearing Donovan's white dress shirt. My dress had been irreparably damaged when I'd shifted into a dragon. God, I couldn't get my head around it. My mother had been a dragon. I was a dragon. My father wasn't. How that came to be and how I'd made it this far in life without knowing the truth was still a mystery to me.

What I did know was that someone had carried me to this room last night and locked me in it. I stood from the narrow bed and tested the door, finding it locked. The walls were cinder block. A toilet and a sink took up one corner of a room that wasn't even as wide as I was tall. At least there was a window. Light streamed in from a narrow one near the top of the outer wall of my cell. I could see the sun was already high in the sky through its double-paned glass. Which meant I'd been asleep for hours.

I briefly entertained trying to escape through that window, but even standing on the bed, I couldn't easily reach it let alone hoist myself up. Even if I could, it wasn't the type of window that opened. I might've tried breaking it, if I had anything to use to do so, but it was so small, I wondered if I could even fit through it. And then there was the question of what I would face on the other side of the glass.

I paced my cell, noticing on my third pass that there was a camera in the corner. Great. Tears started again, and I covered my face with my hands. What had I done? I should have never allowed my father to bring me here. And what would Mason do to get me back? I desperately wanted to send a message to him not to try. I didn't want him putting himself in danger for me, especially when this was all my fault. If I'd just refused to attend with my father and stayed away as Mason had requested, I wouldn't be in this mess.

The lock on the door clicked, and I backed away from it as it swung open. My father walked in, dressed in a fresh suit with a stack of clothes in his hands. "Hello, Reagan."

I didn't respond. My hands shook with my desire to strike him, but at the same time a dark vortex of pain opened in my chest. The father I'd known just a day ago was gone. He'd never existed. Whoever this was in front of me, I didn't know him at all. Maybe I'd never known him.

"I brought some clothes for you. Once we get the paperwork done, we'll get you out of here and back home."

I pressed my lips together. All I had control over was my words, and I would not give any extra to this man.

He sighed. "I had to do it, Reagan. You refused to come work for me, and when you called my bluff and told me you were moving out, I couldn't let you leave. Since your mother died, you were the force of creative energy I needed to keep Bailey Enterprises going, not to mention my key to a long and healthy life. I needed you, and you wouldn't listen to reason. Now you will. Once I buy you back, things will change. You'll learn to obey me."

I swallowed down the lump forming in my throat, not over the sick and twisted future my father had painted for me, but because I couldn't stop thinking about my mother. "Did you ever love her?" I couldn't hold the question back any longer.

"Your mother? Of course I did. She bonded to me. Mating, they call it. I loved her very much. She told me what she was before we married. Showed me her inner dragon. It wasn't until after you were born that I truly fathomed the gift she was to me."

"She didn't die of heart failure, did she?"

"No. It was an accident actually. We went to a business dinner at the home of an acquaintance who was a member of the Order. I had no idea what the Order was back then. He recognized what she was right away but didn't honor my ownership of her because I wasn't an Order member."

Ownership of her? Was that how my father viewed my mother? As something he owned?

"She'd become complacent about living among humans under the peace treaty," he continued. "He poisoned her food with the same magic they use to make these." He thumbed his ring. "She died that night, and they came for her. There was a number she called for paramedics that worked with her kind. Only, I found out later, it was the Order that came for her, meaning to capture her. The poison they fed her, it was only supposed to sedate her. But it worked too well, and she died before they could capture her. I didn't even know what had happened until the Order explained it to me the night Roman invited me to become a member. For years, I truly believed it was a heart defect that killed her. That's what the man who called himself a doctor told me. It wasn't like I could get a second opinion."

If any emotion passed through his face as he talked about the death of his wife and my mother, I didn't see it. He talked about her demise as he might speak of the death of a historical figure, from a distance, with interest but no emotion. Seething, I wiped my tears. "And you thought joining the men who had murdered your wife was a good idea?"

He sighed. "Not at first. The first time they asked me, I turned them down. But the world has changed, Reagan. Everything is twenty-four seven, powered by AI. You're either part of the few who are writing the rules or one of the many pawns in the game they're playing." He thumbed the ring again. "With this, I guarantee the future I built for myself, for us. And you'll be part of it. Together, we'll have so much power, there won't be a single meal in America without a Bailey Foods item in it."

"I don't *want* to be part of it," I said through my teeth.

"You won't have a choice." He looked down at his shoes. "The Order has magic that will make you obey me. It will protect you too. What happened to your mother will never happen to you. The cuff will ensure that."

I scoffed. "A cage without bars."

He stepped forward and tried to put his hand on my shoulder. I jerked away.

"By tomorrow night you'll be back in your own bed and everything will look a lot brighter. Trust me on this."

I looked away, shaking my head. "Do I have a choice?"

He backed toward the door. "Not if you want to live."

Without a doubt, if my future was being my father's robot or a coffin, I would choose the coffin. I turned my back to him and stared out the window. After a few minutes, I heard him open the door.

"Goodbye, Reagan." He slipped out, and the lock engaged behind him.

For a beat, I just stared at the wall, processing everything he'd said. Then Donovan's voice came back to me, *Choose the hunt. Find the oak tree.* My resolve poured into my bones like molten steel.

"Goodbye, Dad."

THE ORDER FED ME TWO MEALS DURING MY STINT IN THE CELL. The meals were simple but thankfully tasted better than I expected based on my surroundings. I ate every bite. I wasn't exactly sure what the hunt entailed, but I was positive I'd need the calories and my strength. My window faced east, so I couldn't see the sunset, but I watched the light fade, both anxious and dreading what came next.

My father had brought me an outfit from my closet—leggings, a sweater, and some booties. No jacket. No part of him expected me to choose the hunt. If it weren't for Donovan, I wouldn't even know I had a choice. I bristled at the thought of him packing this before we left, knowing what he was about to put me through. He'd been planning this from the beginning. I swallowed down the bile in my throat and tried to channel all my anger into an inner battery of energy I could draw on later when I needed it.

The lock clicked and the door opened. I thought they'd send my father for me, but instead, Roman appeared, that wicked smile making my organs shrivel. I took an involuntary step backward.

"I have to admit, I'm tempted to bid on you myself," he said, scanning me from head to toe. "Something tells me it would be a joy bending you to my will."

I kept my mouth shut, hoping he'd lose interest, but he glanced over his shoulder and then sauntered into the room, chucking me under the chin with his knuckle.

"You'd like being under my command, wouldn't you? I can see it in your eyes. You're a woman who needs to be told what to do."

I spat in his face.

Slowly he released my chin, pulled a handkerchief from his suit pocket, and wiped his face with it, never looking away from me. Fuck, his eyes were as black and soulless as a snake's. "Save it for later, *tesoro*. If we start this now, I might leave a mark. How would that go over at auction?"

He grabbed me by the arm and hauled me through the door, which was a relief because every moment alone with him in that cell amped up my anxiety. I was led to a small elevator and then guided back to the ballroom. All the women were gone. I noticed that immediately.

Everyone in this room was a member of the Order. Some were dressed in designer suits, including Roman, his father, and my dad. Others were outfitted for the outdoors—for hunting. Whether someone wore Patagonia or Armani seemed to indicate what they thought would happen tonight. The majority were in suits. Few expected a woman like me to choose the hunt. Both types of men seemed equally excited to be there.

Roman guided me onto the dais where the band had played last night and held me in place beside his father, Stefan. Part of me wanted to kick and scream and claw Roman's eyes out, but I wasn't stupid. My best chance of escape was remaining calm and keeping my wits about me. Losing control would waste valuable energy. I scanned the room and saw Donovan standing by the door, hands folded in front of his hips. I took comfort in his presence even though I now understood why he couldn't help me. My gaze fell to the cuff on his wrist.

Stefan turned toward me. Unlike his son, the older man had kind eyes, as if there was some fragment of a soul left in his body. There wasn't, I was sure. He was the head of the Order after all. The dichotomy made me uneasy. At least Roman looked like the rat-eating snake that he was.

"Reagan Bailey, you've broken the peace treaty between the Saint's Order and dragonkind. The Order retains the right to your person in appeasement for your transgression. Per our tradition and the terms of the accord, we offer you a choice: auction to the highest bidder or to be hunted to your death on these grounds. Which do you choose?"

"The hunt," I answered immediately.

A murmur rippled through the crowd, and Roman's hand gripped my arm tighter.

Stefan shook his head. "I'm not sure you understand," he said, lowering his voice. "You can choose to have a nice life with one of these very wealthy men"—he gestured toward the crowd—"or be hunted like an animal to your death."

I peeled my lips back from my teeth, and when I spoke again, my voice held conviction I wasn't entirely feeling. "I'd prefer to die, thank you. I choose the hunt."

"No!" my father cried. "Reagan, you don't know what you're saying!"

Stefan frowned, those disturbingly soft eyes settling on me and then on Donovan. "The decision is made. Take her to the starting point. Prepare yourselves for the hunt. We begin in twenty."

Roman pulled me toward the door, my father's voice rising. "No! I'll pay anything. She's mine. She's mine!"

No one else said a word. Roman navigated us through the house and out a back door to the edge of a heavily forested yard. The cold lashed at me like a whip, but I wasn't offered a coat. What did the prey need to be warm for? I remembered how Mason was always warm even without a coat and hoped my dragon half would kick in.

"I didn't think this day could get any better." Roman's lips brushed my ear as he whispered into it. "But hunting you down and watching you die will be like frosting on butter cake."

I tucked my trembling fingers into my armpits. "What flavor frosting? They say cyanide smells like almonds. Choke on it."

He sneered, his hand twitching like he wanted to strike me. At that moment though, Stefan stepped into the yard. "Roman, a word?"

Another man came to guard me while Roman snuck off to talk to daddy. I knew I'd regret inciting him, but I couldn't help myself. If I was going to die tonight, I would not do so silently. Which brought me back to my primary objective—not dying. How the fuck was I supposed to find an oak tree out here in the dark?

Weren't they all oak trees? Fuck. Fuck. Fuck. I was doomed.

Men filtered out of the house in their vests and puffer jackets. None of them had guns or arrows that I could see, but if I'd understood correctly last night, their rings could transform into dragon-killing weapons.

Stefan stepped to my side. "You'll be given a thirty-second head start. You can shift, but the enchantment on this property will not allow you to fly beyond its borders. You may go or hide anywhere within it, however." He raised his hand. "Gentleman, at the ready." His eyes shifted back to me, and all the softness was gone. "Begin!"

Chapter Twenty-Nine

REAGAN

Heart pounding in my ears, I sprinted for the widest tree I could see from the house, slipping behind it so that I'd be harder to spot. Once I felt my way was concealed, I ran straight back into the forest as fast as my legs would carry me. My thirty-second lead was barely enough for my eyes to adjust to the dark. I frantically searched the trees for the mysterious oak Donovan had mentioned, but it was hard when I had to keep moving. Already I heard footsteps falling behind me.

What I needed was a better vantage point. If I knew where the oak was in the yard, I could head in the right direction. My wings were useless. Shifting would be too slow and painful to help me now. But I spotted a tree with promise and leaped for its lowest branch. I hadn't climbed one since I was in middle school, but either it was like riding a bike or transforming into a dragon had given me some new skills because I reached the upper branches faster than I'd have ever thought possible, even with the adrenaline rush. Bracing myself, I scanned the forest in both directions.

Crap. I winced when I saw what was coming for me. My heart leaping into my throat. Some of the men had swords that glowed with the same electric-blue light I'd seen in the cauldron. Others had bows and arrows. Still others had crossbows. I didn't see any guns, thank God. A few of them were worryingly close to the tree I was in, and one of the closest was Roman. Donovan had said he was an expert hunter. Could he smell me?

I tried to quiet my breathing, but I was panting so hard it was impossible to stay totally silent. With trembling fingers, I gripped the branch beside me and concentrated on finding the oak. I didn't see the tree, but I did see something else.

A drone hovered about one hundred yards from where I was, as the crow flies. *Thank you, Imani.* I wasn't sure how she knew where I was supposed to go, but who else would be operating a drone out here? I made a mental map of how to get there and started descending from my roost. When I didn't see anyone around me, I dropped to the ground and started to run.

Oof. Something slammed into my back, knocking me forward so that I had to break my fall with my hands before my chest and face slapped the ground. I rolled over to find Roman looming over me with a crossbow in his hands.

I scrambled away from him.

He snatched my ankle and yanked me nearer.

I kicked and scratched, but he wrestled me onto my back, straightened my arms to my sides and knelt on my wrists. He pointed the crossbow directly at my face. I panicked but forced my screams to remain whimpers. I couldn't risk attracting more Order members.

"This won't be quick," he whispered. "I want to watch the light bleed from your eyes." His voice was so cold I questioned whether he was truly human. He lowered the point of his arrow to my stomach.

And that's when a dark figure slammed blue metal into the side of Roman's head. The bastard rolled off me, unconscious, and I glanced up to see my father standing over him with a sword. He'd hit Roman in the head with the hilt. Roman's crossbow had transformed back into a ring when he passed out and was on his finger again as if it never was a deadly weapon.

My father looked both ways, then met my gaze. "Run," he mouthed. "Go."

I scrambled to my feet and sprinted, breathless and bruised from fighting Roman, toward the oak and Imani's drone. My heart leaped when I scented Mason. I was definitely going in the right direction! Mason was here. His scent grew stronger with every step.

I pushed myself faster, although my lungs burned and my muscles protested. And then I saw him standing with his back pressed against an enormous oak tree, another dragon even bigger and broader than Mason in the branches above him. Tears streamed down my face, and I hurled myself toward him.

Ice speared my back, and I screamed, but my momentum carried me into Mason's waiting arms. And then the darkness carried me away.

Chapter Thirty

MASON

Rage changed my vision to red when I saw the arrow pierce Reagan's back. I caught her in my arms and shot straight up, landing in a branch beside my uncle. My blood boiled with my dragon's desire to shift. I had a taste for blood. I wanted to grind the bones of anyone responsible. But Connor's hand landed on my neck.

"We've got to get her out of here. Now," he hissed.

"What about the arrow? It's enchanted. It's killing her!"

"If we remove it here, she'll bleed out. We have to get her to Morwyn."

He was right. Besides, being here was making me itch. Angry voices were gathering below. The Order was realizing their mistake, and they weren't happy about it. I cradled Reagan tightly against my chest and used my power to camouflage us both as I carried her from the property. She was unconscious and so cold her lips had turned blue, but when we arrived at Imani's van, I thanked the creator Reagan was still breathing.

"Jesus Christ, she's got an arrow sticking out of her back! I'm calling 911," Imani said, shoving her drone into the back of the van.

Connor snatched the phone from her hand. "Can't. They'll hurt more than help. We've got to get her to Morwyn."

"Who the hell is Morwyn?" she yelled.

Connor held out his hand. "Give me the keys. I'll drive."

She tossed them to him.

The sound of motorcycle engines drawing near turned our heads. My eyes narrowed.

"Three men with crossbows, incoming!" Imani yelled, rounding the van. "There's a gun in the glove compartment."

"Won't need a gun," I said, gently setting Reagan down in the back of the van. "We're off Order property, right, Connor?"

He nodded. "And they've drawn weapons."

We shifted so fast I barely got my clothes off in time.

"Holy shit. Holy fucking shit," Imani yelled.

We were already airborne. Arrows flew. Connor and I broke apart, and the enchanted steel shot between us, narrowly missing my wing. I barreled for the attacker closest to us, snatched him off his bike with my teeth and sank my claws into his throat. His screams turned to gurgles as I slowly tore his head from his shoulders. Below me, his bike spun out into the ditch.

I spit his head at the second rider, who was frantically reloading his crossbow. He watched the decapitation bounce and roll near his feet, his expression filling with terror as he aimed and pulled the trigger. I hurled the headless body in my claws at the incoming arrow, my dragon laughing as it absorbed the shot and then dropped harmlessly to the pavement. Pouncing, I tore out the shooter's middle, tossing the man's lower half to the opposite side of the road.

A blast of fire channeled beside me, and I saw the third rider melt along with his weapon and his bike. Once Connor's fire stopped, the charred carcass tipped over with the soft creak of bending metal and broke apart into a pile of ash.

We waited a beat, but no one else came. They'd struck quickly, and we'd ended it just as quickly. I shifted back into my human form, threw on my clothes, and leaped into the back of the van beside my mate and Imani. She'd covered Reagan in a blanket and was holding her. I secured the doors and took Reagan into my arms again as Connor started the engine and the van tore out of there.

It took Imani another minute or two to find her voice. "You two are the scariest motherfucking things I've ever seen in my life."

"It's rare we have to defend ourselves like that. We don't normally attack humans."

"Yeah? They had it coming after what they did to

her." She shifted in her chair. "I just wasn't expecting the"—she swallowed—"decapitation."

I pressed my lips to Reagan's forehead. She was warmer now, thank the creator. "I thought you were a photographer for the *Independent*. Where'd you come by a van like this?" The equipment in here was worthy of one of those three-letter government agencies.

She threaded her fingers together across her stomach. "You're not the only ones with secrets."

"You know ours. Now tell me yours."

Leaning forward, she braced her elbows on her knees. "Let's just say I work for an independent agency that's very interested in exposing injustices in our world."

"How long have you known about us?"

Her brow arched. "Since today!" she said as if she truly was surprised by the revelation. "But we've known about them for a while." She gestured toward the house. "We just didn't fully understand their purpose. My employer follows the money. Those assholes have a lot of it and give new meaning to the word *exploitative*."

"Who's your employer?"

Imani didn't answer, just wiped her forehead with her sleeve. I decided not to press. We had more important things to worry about. "You can't tell anyone about us, Imani. If that's going to be a problem—"

A quick inhale parted her lips. "My employer already knows, Mason. Everything we've seen today, they've seen too. But that doesn't mean we'll share your secret. It just means no matter what you do to me

—and believe me, I am terrified of what you might do to me—the genie isn't going back in the bottle. So maybe it would be better if we could all remain friends."

I sniffed her but couldn't smell a lie. Fuck, there went the possibility of wiping her mind.

Reagan moaned, and I stroked her hair. "I'm here. We're going to get you help. Just hang on."

Imani sighed. "Reagan is my best friend. She has been since middle school. I wouldn't do anything to hurt her, and now that you're her... partner—"

"Mate."

"Right... I don't want to hurt you either. I'll make sure the people I work for understand that you guys are on the side of humanity here. Your secret is safe with me, and I expect it will be safe with them as well."

Reagan stirred again in my arms, moaning. Gently I drew back the blanket along with her torn shirt. The arrow had entered near her scapula, and the tip exited just below her right collarbone. Had it been a regular arrow, I'd have guessed it wasn't a fatal hit. But the skin around the wounds was branched with sickly blue-green veins like the cursed magic was spreading.

"We're almost there," I promised her. "I'm going to take care of you."

I banged my fist on the wall between me and the cab. "Faster, Connor."

"Hey, is she going to be okay?" Imani asked, a hint of panic in her voice now that she'd noticed the festering infection too.

I didn't answer her, which probably told her everything she needed to know.

Imani shifted uneasily. "She was going to drop the article, Mason. Pissed me off actually because we had an agreement that we were going to investigate together. She learned at the last second that her father's event was with the Order and had to make a choice. She saw an opportunity to learn about the Order from the inside and asked for my help again. Obviously she didn't realize the danger she was in."

I held Reagan tighter. I couldn't think about that now. All I wanted was for her to be okay. We'd have a lifetime to talk through the why of it, if she made it through this. I released a relieved breath when the van finally came to a stop and I heard the driver's door open.

Imani bounded from her seat and opened the doors for me, and then I was moving, carrying her toward Morwyn and the clinic as fast as I could without jarring her.

The dragon doctor was the same as ever—looming, stoic, intense, his untamed hair and wild hazel eyes giving him a definite Einstein vibe. But the Virgo was meticulous, an unparalleled healer. If anyone could save Reagan, it was him.

At his direction, I carried her inside and straight to a trauma room where I laid her on her on the metal table. A nurse nudged me away and started working on her. Soon a machine registered the pattern of her heartbeats and the nurse was poking an IV into her arm to connect to a bag of fluids. A growl rumbled in my chest.

"Take him outside," Morwyn said to Connor. "We can't have him complicating things."

What he meant was the arrow had to come out, and it was going to hurt, and my mating instinct would cause me to want to kill him and his nurse too, even if he was helping her.

Connor's hands landed on my shoulders. "You heard the doctor."

"I'll call you once we have her in a room," Morwyn promised.

We were almost to the door when my dragon started roaring inside my head. A second later, I heard the alarm on the heart machine blare. Everything in my world narrowed to her. I hardly registered Connor knocking me to the floor or my fists flying at him. He was between me and my mate—that's all that mattered.

The nurse appeared and said something about "enough sedative for an elephant." Connor wrestled my arm into position and she injected me; then he delivered a swift punch to my head. I mellowed out after that.

He propped me up in the waiting room where he murmured, "I can't believe you're still conscious" every twenty minutes or so.

Imani appeared in front of me with a cup of coffee. "It's not as good as yours, but beggars and choosers, ya know."

Connor groaned. "Really? After what we went through to pump him full of sedatives, you're going to offer him a coffee?"

She pursed her full lips. "Look at him. I'm not going

to claim to understand the biology of your species, but it's pretty clear to me that Mason would tear his own arm off rather than sleep right now. He's not causing trouble anymore. At least he can feel a little better while he waits for her to wake up."

I took the coffee from her. "Accurate."

She stayed where she was, standing in front of us with her hands on her hips. "She is going to wake up, right?"

I rolled my eyes up to look at her, but she was staring at Connor, not me.

He groaned. "Dragons have exceptional healing powers. Once they get the arrow out, she should be able to recuperate fairly quickly."

I scowled. "She's only half-dragon, and the curse was already spreading when we brought her in here."

Imani flipped me the finger. "Don't you send that into the universe, Mason Forge. Reagan is bouncing back from this, and you two are going to be so grotesquely happy I won't be able to stand to be in the same room as you most of the time."

I nodded once, praying to the creator that she was right.

Two hours later, I popped out of my chair when Morwyn entered the waiting room, his scrubs covered in blood and his hair curling wildly toward the ceiling. His expression looked grim. My dragon whimpered painfully inside me.

He held up both hands, and I realized I'd moved and was standing extremely close to him.

Connor's palm landed on my chest. "Easy."

"She's stable," Morwyn said, "but still unconscious."

"So, she just needs time to rest?" Connor asked.

Morwyn rubbed the back of his head. "We sort of expected her to be conscious by now. Her vitals look good. She's simply not waking up."

"Why? What's wrong with her?" I ran a hand down my face, terrified at what he might say.

"We don't know." Morwyn frowned. "She's a hybrid. We don't have a ton of data—"

"Can I see her?" My voice sounded weak, ancient.

"Yes. Actually, we're hoping, given your mating bond, that you can help pull her back from wherever she is. It's important. The longer she's under, the higher the risk of... complications."

I was already past him, following the tug behind my breastbone to her room. She was propped up in bed, a bandage where the arrow once was. The IV running to her arm made me edgy, so I took a seat on the opposite side of the bed, next to the steady beat of her heart monitor. No one followed me into the room. At last, I was alone with her.

I held her hand in mine and kissed her fingers, taking comfort in the fact they were warm again, although her face remained tragically pale.

"Reagan, I need you to wake up now." I said it like a command, in the same voice I'd used to test the mating bond.

Nothing.

Fumbling with her limp grip, I squeezed her fingers

tighter. Had she even heard me? Was she in there? "Reagan, come on, baby. You should be healing by now. Wake up and talk to me."

Nothing.

"You're killing me. Come on, sweetheart." I climbed into bed beside her, stretching out with my head sharing her pillow. I wrapped my wing around her. Stroked her arm, her cheek.

Nothing.

I cursed. There was only one thing left in my bag of tricks. "I know I promised not to do this, babe, but I've got to know you're in there."

I closed my eyes and entered her dreams.

Darkness. Smoke. Anytime I entered someone's thoughts, I was prepared for the unexpected, which was why I was surprised to find myself in a familiar place when the smoke cleared. Very familiar. I was standing in Forge's Café and Reagan was sitting at the counter, staring into her empty red cup. It looked like she'd been crying. I approached slowly and slipped behind the counter.

"Can I get you another?" I asked gently.

At first she didn't respond. I wondered if she'd even heard me. But slowly she lifted her gaze to mine. What I saw there broke my heart. Pain. Emptiness. A soul-deep fatigue.

"You came for me."

I wasn't sure if she meant rescuing her from the Order or being here with her in her head, so I simply said, "Yes."

I took her hand in mine, rubbed my thumb lightly over her skin. Her hand felt cold, which told me two things. First, Reagan's mental state was sicker than her physical state. Her hand outside her head was warm, but here inside her thoughts, she was freezing. Second, it was a good thing I'd decided to enter her thoughts, because whatever was happening here was keeping her from waking up. "What can I make you?"

She blinked. "You can't. There's nothing here. It's all gone." Her voice was barely more than breath. "I ruined everything."

"I'm here." I pinched her chin just hard enough to let her know I was real. "Nothing is ruined, Reagan. Cappuccino?"

Her brows dipped in confusion. "Yes."

I turned around and went through the motions of making her coffee, although it was my mind producing it in the cup. I didn't need the machine at all. I just wanted to give her time to process that I was here and I was real, even if we were in a mental construct she'd created.

"I... made a mistake," she said.

I glanced over my shoulder at her when I heard her sob.

"You might have been killed." She covered her mouth with her hand. "All because I was too stubborn to let this story go. I was going to, but then this thing with my father, it just seemed like a once-in-a-lifetime opportunity. And I told myself that the information I gained would help you, but deep inside I wanted to go. I didn't want to give up my dream of breaking the story. Everything between us had happened so fast. And now I've lost my father." She sobbed. "He's not dead, but he might as well be. And my mother is gone. And when I wake up, you'll be gone too."

God, the hurt in her voice tore at my heart. All I wanted was to comfort her, and I was tempted to immediately reassure her. But Reagan was a smart woman. She wouldn't believe me if I simply told her I forgave her. She needed to understand it in her soul or she'd never let this go.

"You scared the hell out of me," I began, choosing my words carefully. "When I heard that you'd put yourself in danger and been captured by the Order, all I could think was that history was repeating itself. I told you before how my father traded his life for my mother's. The Order saw him as more valuable because he was a warrior, a member of the Zodiac Brotherhood.

"The Order viewed his death as a victory. All my life, I've carried that with me, and I told myself I'd never allow myself to love someone that much. Love someone enough to literally put our race at risk to save her." I scoffed and shook my head. "I was terrified to love you. People die when you need them most, even dragons. I didn't want to love you even when my dragon insisted that you were his mate, because loving you meant lowering that shield I'd built around my heart to protect me from the thing that had killed my father, that uncon-ditional love and need to protect. I never wanted to be that hero.

"And then when we did mate, and I knew we were

already bonded, I fought the urge to tell you I loved you. You were human after all, fragile and short-lived, and giving that last bit of myself to you seemed entirely too risky. But no matter how determined I was not to love you, I did anyway. When Connor told me you'd been captured, I realized it was never my choice. I'd loved you from the very beginning. From the moment I first saw you chugging your cappuccino like it was lemonade and talking about how you were going to change the world, I knew that I loved you. I just couldn't admit it to myself. The depth of that love became clear to me when I was surrounded by the Order's arrows. You were running toward me, and I finally understood why my father did what he did. He didn't just die for my mom. He died for himself.

"I would rather die five hundred times than suffer losing you, Reagan. I will *always* come for you. I love you with every bit, every cell, of what I am, and as far as I'm concerned, we're in this life together now. I hope in the future you'll trust me. I hope you'll always keep yourself safe. But what you did is ultimately forgivable. I under-stand that you never believed you were a dragon. Even I didn't know it was possible for you to shift. You didn't know that your father was using you or that he intended to trade you for his membership in the Order. How could you have?" I picked up the cappuccino and slid it in front of her, the foam dragon on top giving her a wink that was only possible in a dream.

She looked at it and then looked at me. "You're not going to leave me?"

I shook my head. "Never. But I'd like you to wake up... so that I can marry you."

She wiped under her eyes, the slightest smile tugging at the corners of her lips. "I thought we had to get permission from the Oracle."

"Not entirely necessary now that you're a dragon, but she gave me her blessing anyway."

Reagan smiled brighter. "What about the brotherhood?"

"I've been invited to ascend to the position. Will it bother you being married to a warrior?"

She shook her head, her expression turning contemplative. "The world needs you. What I saw inside the Order was truly disturbing. What they're doing is wrong. I would be proud to be the wife of a brother."

I leaned across the counter and pressed my forehead to hers. "Then what do you say we get out of here and start the rest of our lives?"

Closing her eyes, she released a shaky breath, her lips twitching upward. "I'll think about it. But first, get the hell out of my head."

I didn't want to leave her, but I obeyed. The smoke moved in, then the darkness, and then I was next to her in bed again, praying to any deity that would listen that she'd follow me out.

"Reagan?" I shook her gently by the shoulder. "Please, baby."

She rolled her head toward me and opened her eyes.

I'd never been a man who cried easily. It had been decades. But a sob erupted when she reached for me. I lifted up on my elbow, stroking her face, her neck, her arms. I kissed her everywhere I touched, worshipping her.

"Mason," she said hoarsely. "Was that real? Were you in my head?"

I felt my cheeks warm. "Sorry. It was necessary. There was no other way."

She sighed, her eyes searching mine. "I'm glad you did. And also, never do it again."

I pressed my lips to hers. "Deal."

Chapter Thirty-One

REAGAN

Two days later, I went home, but not to the house I grew up in. To the cottage. My home was with Mason now. Since my father had become a member of the Order and I was a dragon, I couldn't return to his property without breaching the peace treaty. I found myself propped up on pillows in Mason's bed while he tried to feed me toast.

"If this is too much too fast, I can stay with Imani."

"I want you here," Mason said. "Always. You're my mate. This is where you belong." He held out the toast, and I took a bite and then another. Maybe I was hungry.

Every time he reminded me he was my mate, a sense of relief washed over me. I was still learning to trust in the bond between us, and I supposed it would take time to get used to it. Time was something I needed in more ways than one. My wound throbbed, and the bruises from my ordeal still covered me in yellow and purple spots. I'd recovered faster than a human would under the circumstances, but even the part of me that was dragon had limits. The poison in my blood from the Order's enchanted arrow would take a while to purge from my system.

"I'm glad you said that, because I'm officially homeless. I never signed that lease for Whitman's place, and I can't afford it anyway considering I had to call in to work for the week because I get tired walking to the bathroom."

"I've got you covered."

"Oh, and my car... And Litz! Fuck. Everything is at Dad's."

He snorted from his perch at my bedside. "Have a little faith. Let me take care of you."

"But—"

"I told you, dragons attract abundance. It has to do with what we are," Mason explained. "We're not just muses for the humans around us. Our own creative natures draw wealth from the universe. You'll see. Now that you've tapped into your dragon self, opportunity will knock. Until then, what's mine is yours."

I wasn't sure about the wealth from the universe part, but I could see it was important to Mason to feel like I was taken care of. I could worry about how to pay him back later, once I was healed. Now that I was living here, I could help in other ways. I was a fair cook and wasn't above cleaning. I used to help Carlotta when I was younger.

Thinking about my housekeeper brought my thoughts back to my father. "There's something I haven't told you about the night I was shot."

"What's that?"

"Roman caught me during the hunt. He would have killed me if not for my father. Dad used his weapon to knock Roman out; then he told me to run. If not for him, I wouldn't have made it to you." I'd pushed what happened that night out of my mind at first, unable to reconcile the man who had traded me to my enemies with the man who'd saved me from whatever depraved madness Roman had in store for me that night.

The smile faded from Mason's face, and he set the empty plate down on the bedside table. For a long while, he seemed to contemplate how to respond. "When I met with the Oracle, she mentioned that she had a hard time seeing your past because a darkness surrounded you, keeping you from your true dragon nature."

I squinted at him. "She said that?"

"Although your father was initiated that night into the Order, he knew what you were long before that, and he'd drained your energy. I believe you couldn't fully connect to your inner dragon because somehow that aspect of your soul knew that it wouldn't be safe for you to do so."

"Maybe." It made sense.

"I know that you must feel tempted to think that your father saving you that night means there's a part of him that's redeemable. But only a cancerously ambitious man would join the secret society that murdered his wife. I believe, Reagan, that your father may have saved you that night because he was still hoping to keep you. His entire purpose in tricking you onto Order grounds was to make you his prisoner so that he could continue draining your power indefinitely. When you chose the hunt, he saw that dream fade. The thought of another man taking it from him probably drove him mad. But if you lived, if you somehow escaped, the dream was still a possibility."

I stared at Mason, knowing that his interpretation of events was true and feeling dreadfully sad about it. "You're probably right."

We were interrupted when the doorbell rang. "That would be Imani," he said, the smile returning to his face.

"Imani?" I started to sit up, but he held me in place with one immovable palm to my stomach.

"You stay here. I'll let her in."

I rested back against the pillows, hearing him open the doors and then Imani's voice speaking in hushed tones. Another voice too, male. I couldn't hear what they were saying. A minute later Imani's face poked through the doorway, her body obscured.

"Come in!" I held out my good arm for a hug.

"I have a surprise for you." She entered with a wriggling black mop in her arms.

"Litz!" I gathered him into my side, his tail wagging hard enough to turn his entire back end in circles. "Thank you for picking him up!" I hadn't been sure how I was going to get him now that I couldn't set foot on Dad's property.

She hugged me gently with Litz sandwiched between us. "You're welcome. I also brought you as much of your clothes and things as I could fit in your car. It's parked outside."

"Wow. My dad let you in to do that? I'm surprised he didn't burn it all after what happened."

Her face fell and she rolled her lips together, her brows buckling. "About that. Reagan, I have bad news. Actually, there are men here to see you. They weren't sure where to find you until I went to your house."

I shook my head. "Why are there tears in your eyes? Imani, what's going on?" I gripped Litz tighter.

She stood and two men appeared beside her. "I'll be right outside with Mason if you need me." She slipped out the door.

A police officer and a man in a suit with a thick, plastic-wrapped package under his arm stared down at me. The man in the suit spoke first. "Are you Reagan Bailey?"

I nodded. "Yes."

"This is Officer Cunningham, and I'm Detective Brady. I'm afraid we have some bad news." Looking grim, he handed me a card with his name and contact information. I barely looked at it. "Ms. Bailey, your father was found dead yesterday morning from an apparent suicide."

I sucked in a hard, sharp breath. "Suicide?" I couldn't have heard him right.

"A housekeeper named Carlotta found him hanging by the neck from the second-floor balcony railing when she arrived for her shift. It appeared he threw himself over."

A tear escaped the corner of my eye. "That's... Are you sure?"

"I am sorry to have to share this with you now. We heard about your accident from your fiancé. Carlotta told us that you hadn't been home for several days and your cell phone appears to be out of service."

"I lost it." I swallowed.

"I know this must be difficult—"

"My father wasn't suicidal. Are you sure it was...?"

"There were no other fingerprints. No one else on the security footage. No one else had entered the house."

"Oh. Oh." Tears dribbled from my eyes. Killed himself. Hanged himself.

"His body was taken to Saint Joseph's Morgue. Since you are the next of kin, you'll want to contact them about viewing the body if that's your choice. They'll have a few questions about next steps."

"Next steps?"

He cleared his throat. "Your father's will stated that he was to be cremated. They'll want to know what to do with the ashes. Some people want them for the memorial service, but there are other options."

Memorial service. Jesus. My last memory of my father was him telling me to run from his friends who were trying to hunt me like an animal. Throwing him a memorial was more than my brain could process.

"I'm deeply sorry for your loss, Ms. Bailey."

"Thank you," I said absently.

Brady pulled the thick package from under his arm. "Then there's just his personal effects. If you could sign here, I'll hand these over to you."

I signed the paper he held out to me and took the package, which I now realized was one of those resealable hospital bags. I opened it and gently pulled out a pair of my father's pajamas.

A ring dropped onto the bed near my legs. Breath caught in my lungs when I saw it.

"My father was wearing *this* ring?"

"Yes."

"There wasn't another one? Metal with a cross insignia?"

He shook his head and glanced at the officer behind him, who added, "That's all he was wearing when we recovered the body, ma'am."

A lump formed in my throat. "Thank you. I'll call the morgue."

They left. A few seconds later I heard the front door open and close, and then Imani and Mason were by my side again.

"Do you think they killed him?" Imani asked. "The Saint's Order? Maybe they learned that he helped you escape and took him out."

Mason shrugged. "I don't know. It's possible. The Order is capable of altering security footage."

I shook my head, fingering the ring. "No. He killed himself."

They both looked at me. "After my mother died, my dad took his wedding ring off and put it in his office safe.

I never saw him wear it again. No one even knew it was in there but us."

"So?" Imani asked.

I held up the ring. "This is that ring. He was wearing his wedding ring when he died. It was the only one he was wearing."

"Oh, Reagan." Imani placed a hand over her heart.

"I won't ever know exactly what my father was thinking when he killed himself, but the fact that he was wearing this and not his Order ring tells me he was hoping to send me a message. I think he wanted me to know that in the end he chose us over them."

<h1 style="text-align:center">Chapter Thirty-Two</h1>

MASON

One month later...

"If you catch me, you can have me!" Reagan yelled as she soared through the caverns ahead of me. Her beautiful pink wings were tiny compared to mine, and I could and would easily catch her, but right now I was having too much fun watching her fly.

It had been a hard month for Reagan. It had taken over a week for her body to heal from the damage the Saint's Order did to her. Then Connor and I had helped her learn to control her shift. Maintaining a partial shift, like she was doing right now, was a skill most dragons learned when they were young children. Accomplishing it as an adult was more difficult. I couldn't be prouder of how far she'd come.

During that same time, we'd learned her father had left her everything, effectively freeing all his assets from the hold of the Saint's Order. The house, the land, the company...it was all hers. I'd never forgive Richard Bailey for what he'd done to her, but I'd made peace with the fact that he'd done the right thing in the end. Reagan, however, wasn't at all sure what to do with her newfound wealth—potentially sell it all?—and had been putting off making a decision while she healed and learned about her newfound powers.

She also hadn't given up on stopping the Order. The article she'd turned in to her editor was a carefully worded shadow of the truth that focused on the rings and the Order's influence in Washington, comparing them to Skull and Bones. The few heavily edited video clips Imani had turned over to back up Reagan's conjectures lacked any real teeth.

The sanitized piece had appeased the *Independent* while staying within the bounds of our accord. The Saint's Order deserved far worse. Sometimes she'd have nightmares about the hunt, wake up and mold herself to my side, and promise me she'd take the Order down one day. I believed her. I wanted the same.

I banked right, exhilarated at the feel of the cool wind and sun. March twentieth. My alignment ended today. The extra energy I'd been channeling from the universe had eased off the past few days but not my desire for Reagan. I'd always want her. She was the best part of my every waking hour and the person I longed to dream about.

The ridge where I'd wanted to take her came into

view, and I surged forward, catching her around the waist and guiding her to its ledge. "Gotcha."

She turned in my arms, tucking her wings away. "Finally. Can't you tell when a girl wants to be caught?" she said breathlessly. Her fingers dropped to my fly.

"Wait, I want to show you something." I turned her by the shoulders toward the setting sun. Miles of forest stretched out beyond us toward a breathtaking, orangey-purple sky.

"My god, that's an incredible view."

"Even the best human climbers haven't found this peak. I love it here."

She grinned over her shoulder. "I love it too. Thanks for sharing it with me."

"I wanted to make it memorable." I pulled a ring box from my pocket and held it in front of her, then lowered myself to the ground. "I've learned that humans often do this on one knee." The little gasp she gave and the twinkle in her eye was exactly what I was hoping for. I flipped open the box. "Reagan, we're already bound as mates—will you marry me and be my wife as well?"

She plucked the ring from the box and slid it onto her finger. It wasn't a diamond. I'd learned that Reagan was wary of them not being ethically sourced. But I'd found an expertly crafted piece of labradorite in a gold and sapphire setting that reminded me of her, colorful and unexpected. Original. I watched her closely as she shifted it in the waning light, her eyes widening.

"I don't know, Forge. I'm a very wealthy woman now. Maybe I should demand a prenup."

"Tell me where to sign."

"Aren't you afraid you'll grow sick of me with time?"

"Not even a little bit."

Her eyes locked with mine. "I love the ring."

"Are you going to leave me on my knees all night?"

Her eyes grew hooded. "Oh, I rather like you on your knees."

She squealed as I grabbed the waist of her jeans and yanked her toward me, placing a kiss on her stomach. "Marry me, Reagan."

With her hands on my shoulders, she bent down to plant a kiss on my lips. "Yes. I can't wait to be your wife."

I rolled onto my back and pulled her on top of me for a celebratory kiss. "I should have brought one of the furs from the cave."

She dug her fingers into my hair. "Are you going soft, Forge? Our first night together, you bent me in half with only a tree to hold me up."

"One of my best memories. Don't tempt me."

"Oh, I plan to tempt you. Maybe more than once. Unless chasing me has left you too tired."

A growl tore from my chest, and with a flap of my wings, I had her on her feet and facing the sunrise. "Do you remember what you promised me? That if I caught you, I could have you?"

"Yeah."

"Changed your mind?"

"Never."

I held her to her promise. I'd caught her. She was mine. And I'd be hers until the stars fell from the sky.

Epilogue

ROMAN

Roman Cifarelli was proud of his insatiable thirst for power. Too many people settled for mediocrity. He would settle for nothing less than becoming a god. He was well on his way. His father, Stefan, would be eighty-three this month, and Roman was next in line to rise to the position of Grand Master of the Saint's Order. It wouldn't be long now. Surely his father would retire soon, both as CEO of Cifarelli Enterprises and as grand master, and then Roman would ascend.

And once he was in charge, he'd change everything.

He knocked on the door to his father's bedroom, needing to personally deliver the news he'd come to share. He was surprised to hear two voices on the other side of the door. It was almost two a.m. Who could Stefan be meeting with at this hour?

Several minutes passed and then the door cracked open, his father on the other side, dressed in nothing but a deep amethyst paisley-print bathrobe. Roman narrowed his eyes.

"What do you want, Roman?" Stefan asked gruffly.

"Who do you have in there? I heard voices."

"No one." Stefan glanced down to tie his robe tighter.

Roman's hand shot out and pushed open the door. Donovan stood near the window in nothing but a towel, his confinement bracelet glinting blue against his golden skin. Roman swallowed down his disgust. "Why is Donovan here and not in his cell?"

Face reddening, Stefan grabbed the edge of the door and shoved Roman into the hall, closing it behind him. "These are private matters, Roman. None of your business."

"Are you...?" He couldn't say it. "Have you *been* with him?"

Stefan glanced away, which was all the evidence Roman needed.

"Why are you here, Roman?"

"I've just learned that Richard Bailey committed suicide last night."

Stefan groaned, his gaze turning downcast as he shook his head. "We should have let the girl go. I had a feeling the plan would go south. She was human for all intents and purposes."

"Let her go?" Roman couldn't believe his ears. "She was his offering! We should be punishing Mathieson for not disclosing the landmark on his property. We should have had her blood drained and bottled by now."

The sigh his father released filled him with rage.

"Our treaty with the dragons is precarious, Roman. If we'd killed her, there would be repercussions."

"The repercussion of allowing her to escape was the loss of three members, shredded like barbecue."

"And now one of our newest recruits is dead because we pushed him too far." Stefan rubbed his forehead. "It would have been better to release her. Did someone retrieve Bailey's ring?"

"We attempted to. He must have hidden it before he died. We swept the entire estate, even used a locator spell. We were unable to find it. He was not wearing it when he died."

"And the property? The company?"

"Everything was left to her. It's all hers."

"Jesus. What a mess."

Roman gritted his teeth. "We should retaliate. There should be some recompense for killing our members."

Stefan shook his head. "They were in violation of the treaty when they drew their weapons off society grounds."

Roman's hands shook. "Maybe it's time to violate the treaty then. I'm not the only one in the Order who believes we should break it and go to war again. It's outdated. The world is positively infested with dragons. We need to take back our God-given purpose as a society."

"There will be no retaliation, Roman. That's an order." Stefan turned to reenter his room.

"At least agree to put it to a vote." Roman wanted to climb out of his skin. His father had gone frustratingly soft.

"Go home, Roman. Get some rest." His father's hand landed on the doorknob.

"I won't be so easily dismissed," Roman said, seething. "You can deny me this now, Father, but in a few years, you'll step down and I'll be grand master, and it will happen anyway. You're only delaying the inevitable."

Stefan turned a steely gaze on him. "Then I will never step down. Goodbye, Roman." He slipped inside his room and shut him out.

Roman's hands balled into fists and something dark, something he kept buried deep within him, wriggled toward the surface. He would not be dismissed so easily. He would not allow his dragon loving father to dishonor the Saint's Order with his blasphemous, weak leadership.

"You'll step down," he promised through his teeth toward the closed door. "Or I'll take you down."

THANK YOU FOR READING LEGACY OF FIRE. IF YOU ENJOYED this title, please leave a review wherever you buy books.

Mason and Reagan are hoping for a happily ever

after, but relations with the Saint's Order are growing increasingly tense, especially when Mason's Uncle Connor steals Roman's bride from the altar! Continue the story with DRAGON ASCENDING, available now!

Or turn the page to read an excerpt—>

Sneak Peek: Dragon Ascending

Prologue

Fontaine Saint-Michel, Paris, France

American photographer Lucy Vale adjusted her camera case on her shoulder, annoyed to find herself alone in front of the Fontaine Saint-Michel. She glanced at her watch. Four in the morning, as instructed. If her client weren't an eccentric billionaire who'd prepaid in cash for this shoot, she'd never have taken this job. But when a man offers you four times your regular rate plus a free trip to Paris for a super-secretive one-hour gig, it's hard to say no.

Still, it annoyed her—the hour, the lateness, the entitlement.

She groaned when she finally spotted him walking toward her under the streetlights, the only thing moving aside from the occasional car zipping along the boulevard. The plaza was oddly silent, although she didn't frequent Paris enough to know if that was common at this hour.

As he strode closer, she recognized him from his picture. *Pictures* actually. And videos. That was the thing about running a global empire, she supposed. He'd spent his share of time under the microscope of journalists everywhere.

But then she glimpsed his outfit. Shook her head. Not what they'd agreed to by a long shot. "Have you brought a change? Your dark clothing will get lost in this light. I'm not a miracle worker."

"I know what you are, Lucy." A jagged blade appeared in his hand, lighting up and casting an otherworldly blue glow between them.

"What do you have there?" Lucy glanced between the sculpture of the archangel Michael vanquishing the devil that formed the pinnacle of the Fontaine and the prop in his hand. So that was it then. This was to be a nerdy fantasy-world thing. "Oh, like the statue! Well, we can try it, but at this hour I can't guarantee I can achieve the results you're looking for."

He reached her, his lips drawing back off his teeth in a chill-inducing smile. A smile that made Lucy's skin tighten and her deepest instincts compel her to run. But it was too late for that.

His gloved hand closed around her throat, cutting off her scream.

"Oh Lucy, I guarantee you will provide exactly the results I'm looking for."

Chapter One

CONNOR

"Jessie, if you burn that sauce, I swear on my father's grave you'll be on tomorrow's menu." My new saucier came highly recommended, but as the owner and head chef of Diabolique gastropub, I have high standards. I run my kitchen like a war room. My staff are my soldiers. Every evening, I wage a battle to serve as many hungry people as possible the most absolutely showstopping meals this kitchen can pump out.

Doesn't hurt that I'm also a dragon and can smell the sauce starting to curdle from six feet away.

Jessie lifts the pan off the burner and stirs vigorously. "Got It, Chef!"

I love nights like this. The bustle. The verve. The spark. Most of the humans working in my kitchen don't realize they're feeding off my dragon energy, growing as culinary artists thanks to a celestial gift the creator sent them thousands of years ago. Dragons like me coexist in secret with humans in order to inspire them, to help evolve their species to its ultimate potential. Diabolique has the reputation of being a proving ground for up-and-coming talent. The magazines and influencers think it's because I'm some great mentor, and I'm no slouch in that department, but it has far more to do with being a dragon. The magic in my skin is working on my staff every day they're here.

In a year, I predict Jessie will be running his own kitchen, and that's all right by me.

The door to the front of house swings open, and a four-foot-eleven-inch fireball of a woman with curly gray hair and a neck tattoo appears in front of me. Carmen is my manager, an Army veteran and grandmother of four whom I keep around because nothing fazes her. Nothing. There could be a shootout on the floor and she'd find a way to calmly usher the customers into the alley to finish their meal *Lady and the Tramp*–style. She's also one of the few humans who knows what I really am.

Tonight her fists are on her hips, her spine rigid enough to add two inches to her height, and her lip is curled the way it does when she's seriously annoyed.

"What happened?" I plate the fish I've been poaching and give her my full attention.

"Table seven wants to speak with the chef."

Everyone stops. For a heartbeat, her words hang in the air. Even the burners on the stoves seem to pause, their flames bending in her direction like they can't believe their ears. The saucier stops whisking. My sous-chef stops dicing. My entire kitchen staff seems to hold their collective breath.

Long ago, I gave up being offended by this reaction. My temper is renowned to the humans in this kitchen. And while none of them but Carmen knows I'm a dragon, they all know I'm an Aries. What you see is what you get and I never back down from a confrontation.

"Table seven." It's the end of the night, but I pride myself on every dish that leaves this kitchen. And I remember every order. "What's wrong with the steak?"

"He says it's overcooked." Carmen tosses her hands as if the notion is preposterous, and it is. There's a reason I hired her despite her advanced age. She isn't afraid of anything, including me, and she doesn't suffer fools.

Tossing my apron onto the counter, I pass her, mumbling that I'll take care of it, and march to table seven. I'm big. Around six foot five and ripped thanks to my dragon genetics plus warrior training regimen. The humans I meet often joke I'd make a good linebacker with my general width, which Carmen says is like two average guys standing side by side. I don't know about that, but I make no effort to diminish my otherworldly attributes as I approach this customer. No. I plan to intimidate this asshole until he's near wetting himself.

The man's gaze locks on to my crossed arms first, then traces up and up and up to meet my eyes. *Yeah, way the hell up here, buddy* my expression conveys. *You ready to tango? Because I was born knowing the steps.* It's then that I notice his date. Interesting. This guy is a four at best, but his girl is a strong eight. Her gaze travels north along my torso in the same way, but her eyes hold more than a little heat when our gazes connect. I flash her a lopsided smile. Her brows lift.

"You asked to see the chef?" I mumble, forcing my attention back toward the man.

"You're the chef?" he asks incredulously.

"Connor Drexler," I say by way of introduction. I don't offer my hand. "What can I do for you?"

He swallows, puffing up his chest. "My steak is overcooked."

I glance at the bright red middle of the piece of meat on his plate. "How rare do you want it?"

"Rare rare. This is clearly medium rare."

I stab a finger toward his meal. "If that beef was any rarer, there would be hoofprints leading to your table."

He crosses his arms and leans back in his chair.

Across from him, his date shifts nervously, her lashes fluttering. "It looks rare to me, Richard."

"No one asked for your opinion," the man barks, like she's a dog he means to redirect.

I picture my hand shooting out, cuffing his ear, and knocking him out of his chair. I know guys like this. He's a little man in a designer suit, a modern Napoleon type, making up for his small stature by throwing money around along with his attitude.

"Oh, I'm very interested in her opinion," I say, returning her smile with a small, lazy one of my own. My voice drops an octave as I add, "on a number of things."

"Hey, asshole, what about my steak? You gonna fix this or what?"

A low growl rumbles in my chest, and my skin grows hot with the desire to turn this fucker inside out. My bones rattle with a growing lust for his blood. They actually rattle as if I'm standing too close to an arriving train. I'm fantasizing about dismembering this guy and then bending his girlfriend over his bloody remains and giving her what I see she wants when she looks at me with those bedroom eyes.

Thank the creator, Carmen chooses that moment to deliver a swift punch to my kidney as she passes behind me. I do a double take.

"Check the date and time, Chef," she says. "And stop making that noise."

I glance at my watch. Past midnight.

March twenty-first.

My dragon's alignment.

Fuck.

"Are you wearing contacts?" The woman at the table leans forward, catching my eye.

Yeah, I bet she got a show. I need to get out of here before I do something I'll regret.

"Uh, Carmen?" I call her back over from the hostess stand.

"Chef?"

I close my eyes for a beat while I rein in my inner beast, then give her a nod. "Guy wants a rare steak," I mumble. "Can you give him the Bones treatment?"

"It would be my pleasure." She grins wickedly, then grabs his plate and follows me back into the kitchen.

Bones is my German shepherd. Recently he's started

getting really picky about his kibble. I've figured out if I put his bowl on the counter, shake it a bit to stir it up, then put it back in front of him, he eats it. It's about the attention, not the food.

Carmen will let the guy's steak sit under the warmer for fifteen minutes, flip it over, trim it, and rearrange it on a new plate, then bring it back out to him. By that time, I predict table seven will either eat it or bolt.

Meanwhile, I need a breather to make sure my dragon knows who's boss. I cut left and head into my office, bracing myself on the desk and taking a deep, cleansing breath. Every dragon is born under a certain star sign. Mine is Aries. But unlike humans, when a dragon reaches the part of the year aligned with his sign, we undergo changes. It's the only time of year when we're fertile, and so our dragons are at their strongest and most virile during that month. But all that power comes at a price. We run hot, all our emotions razor-sharp and our needs exaggerated to a fine point. Hunger feels like starvation. Anger feels like an explosion. And lust—fuck, we have a special name for it. *Appetency,* mating sickness.

Every year we grow older, our appetites get stronger. For those of us lucky enough to find a mate, our alignment ceases to be a problem. But without our one and only, our need grows and grows until, around the age of a hundred, we literally go up in flames. I'm thirty-eight, and I haven't found a mate yet. Right now my spleen feels like it's sliding down a red-hot cheese grater, and my dragon is telling me that the only thing that will ease the pain is seeing blood or sinking deep into a pretty pink pussy.

Fuck.

I'm still doing the mindful-breathing thing when the phone rings—the old landline. I flip the handset into my palm and bark, "Connor."

"Why aren't you answering your cell?" Seb's voice comes down the line, skating between anger and annoyance. He's my best friend and a dragon warrior like me. A Taurus.

"Because I'm busy running a restaurant. The phone's a distraction. I turn the ringer off while I'm working." I reach for it now, noticing the screen is filled with missed calls from the Zodiac Brotherhood, the group of warrior dragons like me who've taken an oath to defend our kind.

"Right now you need to be distracted. Way distracted. Distract yourself immediately, feel me?"

"What's going on?"

"Check CNN. News coming out of Paris. You're not going to like it, bro."

Deep dread rises like bile as I scroll to the news app on my cell. This is the worst time for something to happen that involves the brotherhood. Our Pisces brother, Solomon, has to step down for personal reasons, and my nephew Mason is taking his place. Only the transition isn't complete because removing Solomon from his position while the wheel of the celestial year was in Pisces would have put us all at risk. We've scheduled an ascension ceremony to take place in one month, at the end of my alignment. The timing gives Solomon plenty of time to train his replacement and gives Mason a year to get up to speed before he's put in a leadership position. Only problem is, the transition to my leadership literarily happened tonight at midnight. And for the next four weeks, we'll be down a dragon in the brotherhood. Solomon is gone, but Mason hasn't ascended. And I'm in the throes of adjusting to an influx of power that feels like it might snap me in two.

It's a fucking terrible time to have an incident.

A story labeled BREAKING NEWS: PHOTOGRAPHER LUCY VALE FOUND MURDERED is at the top of my news app. I tap on the included video.

"Horror in Paris," the news anchor announces. "Award-winning photographer Lucy Vale was found dead in front of the Fontaine Saint-Michel in the early-morning hours by a passing tourist, her body brutally mutilated. Police suspect cult activity as sections of her back were flayed and stretched to look like wings. Amateur video shows an inscription, '*Astra inclinant, sed non obligant,*' written in her blood at the crime scene. Experts tell us it's Latin for *the stars incline us, they do not bind us.* French police are seeking any eyewitnesses to this very public murder."

"*Astra inclinant, sed non obligant.*" Every dragon knows that phrase. It's the motto of the Saint's Order, the organization of wealthy humans who are sworn to kill us. They all have it engraved on their rings, a historical slap to dragonkind who come from the stars and are guided by celestial energy. It's basically the Order's way of saying fuck direction from the universe and the connection between all living creatures; we are the gods here and we'll take what we want when we want it.

"Yeah," Seb growls. "If an Order member didn't do this, it's a great fucking copycat."

"Her wings weren't even developed. She wasn't a dragon." My inner beast rages.

"Her dad is half. I met the man once. He couldn't shift, which means Lucy was a dormant."

"Did she even know about her heritage? The Order?"

"I don't know. I don't think so."

"Why the fuck would they do this?"

"I'll tell you why. It's an act of war, that's what it is! Carving up one of our civilians on public soil? It's egregious." The smoky timbre of Seb's dragon rises with his anger. There's a reason the sign for Taurus is a bull. He's as hardheaded as they come. Once he places the blame, no one can convince him otherwise. Honestly, in this case I agree with him.

I brace myself on the desk, everything in me wanting to avenge Lucy's death. *Bite. Shred. Kill,* my dragon growls from inside, wanting control. "Someone's got to pay for this."

Rustling comes down the line, and I picture Seb smoothing the arms of his suit jacket. I know that sound. He's wrangling his dragon into submission. "As much as I'd love to get behind immediate retaliation, you know we can't do anything rash. We'll have our day, but we need to be patient. Follow the process. The sun is in Aries, Connor."

"You think I don't know where the wheel is?" I snap. "For fuck's sake, I almost took off a customer's head today so I could fuck his girlfriend in a pool of his blood. Believe me, I know it's on me." Normally Solomon would gradually transition the reins to me acting as a consultant as the wheel turned from Pisces to Aries, but because the Oracle directed him to step down immediately and focus on training Mason, he's unreachable. I'm going to have to jump into this headfirst.

"Okay, then you know it's your duty to summon the four."

By *the four*, Seb's referring to the next three Zodiac Brothers in the wheel as well as me. It's been a long-standing tradition in the brotherhood. We're at our strongest during our alignment. The brotherhood is composed of one warrior dragon born in each of the twelve sun signs so that we always have one brother with exceptional power to lead. But because that power wanes with the passage of time, the Oracle requires the next three positions in the wheel to be in agreement on any major decisions. That means that while I am technically calling the shots at the moment, Seb as our Taurus, Remus as our Gemini, and Ellison as our Cancer have to agree for me to pull the trigger on any major response. Seb and I are close. Remus is easily swayed. But Ellison?

"Fuck. I know technically I'm supposed to, but you know Ellison will drag his feet. That asshole has never met a risk he's willing to take."

Seb grunts in agreement. "He only gets one vote. As long as we can sway Remus, we're good. But that would be easier if we had additional evidence. Do you think you can reach Donovan?"

Donovan is the reason we have the peace accord to begin with. Fifty years ago, the Libra brother sacrificed himself in exchange for the Order's promise to stop hunting and trapping dragons on land that isn't owned by the Order. Now he serves as the grandmaster's personal good-luck charm, the Order's own dragon prisoner, and the source of the blood used in the spell to make their weapons. He communicates with us rarely and only under great risk to himself.

"I'll try his burner. He was able to get a message through a few weeks ago. He might know what's going on."

"It's a start. We need confirmation that the Order is behind the murder before we retaliate, or we could be throwing the peace accord and everything Donovan has worked for out the window."

"Thank you, Captain Obvious. I'm on it."

"Only trying to help. Believe me, all I want to do is track the killer down and show him what happens to Order members who touch our civilians. I recommend starting at his toes and seeing how many parts we can tear off before he dies."

My dragon twists in my torso, loving that idea. I rub the back of my neck. "Consider yourself called, Seb."

"Where and when?"

"My place. We need to stay on-world or I won't get Donovan's response to my message. Be there tomorrow night. Eight sharp."

"I'll call my pilot and tell him to ready the jet."

I brace myself on the desk, images of Lucy Vale's desecrated body burning in my mind. "Tell me we're going to kill the fucker who did this."

Seb answers with a growl. "Fuck, yeah. I swear it to the creator."

Chapter Two

FIONA

What a day to oversleep! I stride as fast as I can toward the bistro, feeling hungover despite having not touched a drop last night and hoping that my friend Vivian hasn't given up on me. I'm almost twenty-five minutes late for our lunch date. I practice my apology in my head as I turn the corner and navigate toward the patio. Her latest text says she's already chosen a table outside in the sun.

Vivian's smile cuts through the crowd. She raises a massive glass of red wine and waves me over to an annoyingly wobbly table for two. I leave my jacket on as I take the seat across from her. It's sunny but on the cool side. Typical weather for the south of France at the end of March.

"Sorry, Viv. I set my alarm but slept right through it."

"C'est la vie." She waves a perfectly manicured hand

through the air, her sleek black hair falling over one shoulder. "You're in the south of France. Kick back, relax."

I breathe a sigh of relief that she's not cross. "Thanks for understanding. Even the French Riviera isn't enough of an excuse for how late I am."

"Honestly, if the worst thing I have to do today is sip wine at this bistro for a half hour waiting for a friend, it will be a good day." She demonstrates the wine sipping, and I'm convinced she wasn't put out by my tardiness.

"That's what I love about you, Viv, always looking on the bright side."

The corner of her mouth lifts. "So... are you sure you're late because the alarm didn't go off? Or did that new billionaire fiancé of yours require your attention this morning?"

I give a theatrical gasp at her probing question and clutch invisible pearls around my neck. "Vivian! I don't kiss and tell."

"What good is it being best friends with a romance author if you can't discuss the steamy parts?" Her eyes fixate on my left hand. "Oh my God, is that the ring?"

I hold the new edition to my left hand out and wiggle my fingers so that the diamond catches the light. She gives a long, low whistle. The thing's an iceberg. "Honestly the largest diamond I've ever seen in my life. The American man at the neighboring table looked twice at it like he thought it might be ice for his flat water."

"It's enormous!"

"Roman had it specially designed."

"Right after he hired a bulldozer to carry it to the jeweler. Fuck, your hand must get tired." Viv snorts.

I bite my lip to keep from following that train of thought. Any woman would be proud to have a ring like this, and I refuse to let on that I'm anything but grateful. But no way would I have ever picked this ring for myself. It catches on everything, and I've cut myself on it twice. As soon as I'm married and enough time has passed, I plan to store it permanently in my jewelry box. I change the subject so I'm not tempted to complain. "Thanks for agreeing to be my maid of honor on such short notice.""

"Your relationship has moved fast! From first date to engagement in a month. I've had car repairs that took longer."

Our server arrives, and I point to the wine I want to order, then to a dish with *canard* in the name because I know it means duck. Vivian fills in for me in fluent French.

"When are you going to learn French, woman?" she asks. "Once you're married to a jet-setter, it would help to speak a second language."

"I'll get right on that."

She plants her elbows on the table and rests her chin on her threaded fingers. "Now, about this morning and why you were late..." She bobs her eyebrows.

I roll my eyes. Vivian and I share a publisher, which is how we met. I've made my career in thrillers, specifically the Alex Rogue series about a retired military police officer who is now a private investigator specializing in crimes committed by fringe religious orders and secret societies. Vivian writes steamy contemporary romance.

I know that look in her eye. She wants all the details.

"Sorry to disappoint you, but Roman did not keep me in bed this morning." I laugh. "Actually..." I hesitate to tell her this part because she won't approve. "We've decided to sleep in separate bedrooms until the wedding night."

She narrows her eyes as if she can't quite get her head around what I'm saying. "Wait... is this a recent thing, or are you saying you two haven't, um..." She hooks her fingers together.

"Nope," I admit, toying with my crucifix necklace absently. "He's old-fashioned. Wanted to be married first."

"Oh." She frowns. "That's... weird."

I shrug. "Is it? Old money and old-fashioned?" I laugh. "Maybe I'm more open to it having been raised Catholic. His family seems really conservative. I think it goes with the territory."

She takes a long sip of wine. "But, I mean, he's not like a virgin or anything?"

I laugh. "No." And neither am I, but then she knows that. I don't share that Roman's been so busy with work that I haven't even seen him in two days. "Honestly, I just overslept. I'm exhausted. Planning this wedding, the dress, the flowers, the cake, it's taken a lot out of me even with the hired help."

Vivian's face falls. "Do you think it's your fibro?"

"Don't say its name out loud. I don't want to tempt the universe with the wedding tomorrow."

Her eyes fill with pity. I hate that. I can take anything but pity. "I don't want to jinx you, but after what happened before…"

She means the first time I had a full-blown fibro attack, after Marion was killed and my central nervous system seemed to go haywire with my grief. I'd pushed myself too hard and ended up in bed for weeks. I flatten my napkin on the table with my palm. "It's possible. This whirlwind relationship, the travel, the wedding planning, it's all stressful. Not to mention I haven't been able to write in months."

Her eyes widen. "Still?"

"Not a word."

She lowers her voice as if there's an editor spying on us from a neighboring table. "Wasn't your latest Alex Rogue manuscript due, like, months ago?"

I'm relieved when my wine arrives, and I take a fortifying sip before answering. "Try a year. They gave me an extension following the accident, but my writer's block isn't getting better. First I thought it was because I was grieving Marion, but now I just feel like I can't hear Alex anymore. It's like she's chained up inside my head and refusing to have any further adventures. I haven't been able to write anything more creative than a grocery list in a year. I've tried over and over to start *The Milkmaid*. The story is just *gone*."

Her brows sink. "Oh, Fiona. I'm so sorry." She reaches

across the table and squeezes my hand. "Grief is a powerful emotion. Losing a sister like you did…" she shakes her head. "It makes sense that it might take up all the room in your head. I'm sure your writing voice will return once you have some peace and quiet in your life, room to heal."

I nod. "After the wedding. I'm sure of it."

"But it does beg the question." She leans back in her chair and studies me.

"What question?"

"Everything's happened so fast with you and Roman. The travel, the gifts, the overwhelming publicity of dating a billionaire. Are you sure about this marriage?"

I almost blow a sip of water across the table. "I better be sure. The wedding's tomorrow."

"But… Please don't take this the wrong way. You and Roman moved *very* quickly." She pins me with a knowing look.

"Four weeks from the time he bumped into me at a bookstore to the night he proposed in a hot-air balloon over Paris. Now here we are, wedding in the south of France. Am I sure I want to marry a handsome billionaire who swept me off my feet and proposed with a diamond ring the size of Plymouth Rock? Yes, Vivian, I am."

My attempt at humor doesn't earn her smile.

"Do you love him, Fiona?"

I glance away, wishing the server would interrupt us. "Why else would I be marrying him?"

She squints at me. Sees through me. Damn it. Vivian knows me too well.

I pinch the bridge of my nose and decide I owe her an honest answer. "Look, I get that the romance writer in you wants a big love story with instant chemistry and explosive feelings. You want Roman to be my Henrik Angel." I purposefully use Alex Rogue's on-again, off-again love interest to drive home the point that this is full-blown magical thinking. "But love like you read about doesn't exist. Roman is a solid option. I'm confident my feelings for him will grow with time."

She gapes at me. "No. No. No. Fiona, that's not why you should marry someone."

"Hmmm." I rub my chin as if I'm seriously contemplating her warning. "Well, it's enough for me." When she huffs in response, I lean toward her. "Let me tell you what I *love* about Roman. He can support me, which I need because my sales are officially in the toilet. I'll have health insurance when my fibro makes it impossible for me to get out of bed, and I'll be able to afford the best doctors, nutritionists, and physical therapists once I'm married to him. Oh, and I'll be able to pay off that property Marion loved so much, literally the last piece of her I have in my life. As it is now, I'm barely keeping my head above water. This engagement is a lifeline."

Now she scowls like she smells something bad. "Oh Fiona... you know what I think?"

I'm afraid to ask. "What?"

"I think that life has handed you a raw deal. I think you're marrying Roman because he asked. I think the trauma of losing your sister has made you feel like you have no control over your life, and so you've fallen into a pattern of reacting rather than directing what happens to you. I think your lack of agency over your own life is the reason you haven't been able to write as Alex Rogue since the accident. Alex had agency. She was a woman who made things happen. I think you're marrying Roman because he's an easy answer to your problems, but maybe you need to find your inner Alex again. You're about to bind your life to this man. This man you hardly know. This man you don't love."

I shift uncomfortably in my chair, my skin feeling too tight beneath her scrutiny. I'm saved when the food arrives. "I'm not one of your characters, Vivian. Stop analyzing my motivations. My reasons for marrying Roman are... complex. Far more complex than because he asked. I love the idea of having a family again. Roman is very close to his father and Donovan."

"Who's Donovan?"

"He's this man who is literally always with his dad, Stefan. Roman says he's just a friend. His father's best friend. Like an uncle, I guess."

Vivian cuts into her steak, suddenly wide-eyed. "As much as I am now painfully curious about the 'very close friendship' of the elder Cifarelli, let's get back to you and Roman. Before I stand behind you at that altar tomorrow, I need to know that you're not making a huge mistake. What else besides financial security makes you believe this marriage will work?"

I expected Viv would have questions. As writers and introverts, we live relatively isolated lives and aren't the type of friends who see each other or even chat every day. Admittedly, I've been sparse with her on the details of my relationship with Roman because I didn't want this type of scrutiny. But considering she flew all the way to France to stand up in our wedding, I owe her an explanation.

So I think about my time with Roman and what drew me to him. "He's hardworking and seems to genuinely care about me. I mean, he came on strong and pursued me like no man ever has before. Oh, and he's read all my books. That's how we met. He recognized me in a bookstore and told me he's a huge Alex Rogue fan. Read the entire series. I know you mean well and you want me to say I'm head over heels for this guy, but honestly, our story is more of a slow burn. You are right about one thing though—Marion's death changed me. Since the accident, I don't have the magic like before, not about anything. Maybe you're right. Maybe I am reacting to what's in front of me. Maybe I'm going along with where the universe drags me. So what. I'm tired Vivian. I can't have the type of feelings you're talking about with Roman because I'm not capable of them right now. Perfect doesn't exist, and I don't have the fight in me to wait for it anymore. This is what I want. It's what's best for me."

With a slow shake of her head, she studies her food, pushing it around her plate with her fork. "It's not what I'd want for myself, but you're an adult and you know what's best for you. You could do worse than marrying a billionaire superfan who seems to adore you," she says sternly. "Tomorrow you'll be married. Once things settle down, your muse will return, you'll finish *The Milkmaid*, and all the magic will be back in your life."

I raise my glass. "From your lips to God's ears."

Dear Readers,

Welcome to the world of the Zodiac Dragon Brotherhood. Legacy of Fire is an introduction to a new world and a coming series that will feature a team of twelve dragon warriors who defend the dragon race against the Saint's Order. Each book will feature a warrior in his alignment and his potential mate during a time of increasing tensions with the Order.

The idea for this series came to me last year when I was visiting the Fontaine Saint-Michel in Paris. The sculpture depicts an angel holding a wicked-looking sword, stepping on the back of a dragon-like man. It's supposed to depict good triumphing over evil, but the more I studied that statue, the more I noticed that only the angel had a weapon and armor. Was the dragon truly the devil? Or was this a depiction of a war between two entities that had been completely misunderstood by the artist?

By the time you read this, DRAGON ASCENDING will be available. The opening scene takes place in front of the Fontaine Saint-Michel and kicks off Connor's action-packed story. I hope you'll continue along with me in this series. I have so much more to share.

Love is the truest magic and the most fulfilling fantasy.
Until we meet again,

Genevieve Jack

USA Today bestselling and multi-award winning author Genevieve Jack writes wild, witty, and wicked-hot paranormal romance and romantic fantasy. She believes there's magic in every breath we take and probably something supernatural living in most dark basements. You can summon her with coffee, wine, and books, but she sticks around for dogs and chocolate. Her novels feature badass heroines, fiercely loyal heroes, and fantasy elements that will fill you with wonder. Learn more at GenevieveJack.com.

Do you know Jack? Keep in touch to stay in the know about new releases, sales, and giveaways.

facebook.com/AuthorGenevieveJack

instagram.com/authorgenevievejack

bookbub.com/authors/genevieve-jack

tiktok.com/@Genevievejackbooks

The Zodiac Dragon Brotherhood

Legacy of Fire

Dragon Ascending

Dragon Chained

Dragon Entwined

The Treasure of Paragon

The Dragon of New Orleans, Book 1

Windy City Dragon, Book 2,

Manhattan Dragon, Book 3

The Dragon of Sedona, Book 4

The Dragon of Cecil Court, Book 5

Highland Dragon, Book 6

Hidden Dragon, Book 7

The Dragons of Paragon, Book 8

The Last Dragon, Book 9

The Angel of Paragon, Book 10

The Three Sisters Trilogy

The Tanglewood Witches

Tanglewood Magic

Tanglewood Legacy

A Shadow's Bargain Series

A Bargain With The Shadow Prince

Battle for the Shadow Prince

Bartered by the Shadow Prince

Bride of the Shadow King

His Dark Charms Duet

Lucky Me

Lucky Us

Knight Games

The Ghost and The Graveyard, Book 1

Kick the Candle, Book 2

Queen of the Hill, Book 3

Mother May I, Book 4

Logan (companion novel)

The Wolves of Fireborn Pack Trilogy

Fated Bonds

Feral Instincts

Forever Mated

www.ingramcontent.com/pod-product-compliance
Lightning Source LLC
Chambersburg PA
CBHW011412310726
48972CB00011B/2949